Stone Hard SEALs

SABRINA YORK

DEDICATION

For Carrie, Carmen and Fedora.

ACKNOWLEDGMENTS

My deepest appreciation to Dar Albert for a rocking cover—always gorgeous—and to Carrie Jackson and Fedora Chen for your editing genius.

My heartfelt appreciation to my fellow writers for their support. Especially Cindy Dees, Delilah Devlin, Anne Elizabeth, Sharon Hamilton, Cristin Harber, Elle James, Cat Johnson, Gennita Low, Patrice Michelle, Teresa Reasor and Paige Tyler, for giving birth to Hot Alpha SEALs which, in turn, gave birth to Stone and Drake.

And of course a shout-out to my amazing support team, Linda Bass, Crystal Benedict, Stephanie Berowski, Crystal Biby, Kris Bloom, Kim Brown, Sandy Butler, Carmen Cook, Celeste Deveney, Tracey A. Diczban, Shelly Estes, Lisa Fox, Rhonda Jones, Denise Krauth, Barbara Kuhl, Angie Lane, Tracey Parker, Laurie Peterson, Tina Reiter, Hollie Rieth, Regina Ross, Sandy Sheer, Kiki Sidira, Sheri Vidal, Sally Wagoner, Deb Watson, Veronica Westfall and Michelle Wilson, as well as the shy ones, Christy, Elf, Fedora, Gaele, Lisa, Nita and Pansy Petal.

To all my friends in the Greater Seattle Romance Writers of America, Passionate Ink and Rose City Romance Writers groups, thank you for all your support and encouragement.

Book One:

RYDER

CHAPTER ONE

Lily Wilson braced herself against the railing and tipped her face up to the sun, soaking in the heat. The sky was a shimmering azure and specked with puffy white clouds. The sea was calm. Tiny tufts crested the waves, caught by the briny breeze. Quite a difference from yesterday.

Yesterday a monsoon had pounded the Gulf of Aden, sheeting rain in an impenetrable curtain and tossing their ship like a giant's plaything. The boat was hardly small, with three masts and a thirty-man crew, but the storm hadn't cared. Lily and her friend Brandy had holed up in their cabin, alternately retching and hanging on for dear life. Yesterday, going out on deck would have been insanity. She would have been swept overboard in an instant.

Lily grinned, filled with exhilaration. Yes, it had been miserable and frightening and horrifying at times, but how exciting. Totally at the mercy of Mother Nature, unsure where the next wave might hit. Buffeted and tossed and flung about.

Magnificent.

The name of their ship was apt. The *Avonturier*. The Adventurer. She felt like one.

"There you are," Brandy grunted as she came up to the rail at Lily's side. Her short brown bob was askew and she had pillow marks on her cheek. She wore the same t-shirt she'd worn as they'd hunkered in their bunks. The last couple days must have hit her hard; it was out of character for Brandy to have so much as a hair out of place.

"Good morning to you too," Lily said, nibbling back her smile. It was, perhaps, inappropriate to be amused, but Brandy was still a little green about the gills. Lily couldn't help it. It was fun to see her usually unruffled friend knocked off-kilter.

"I can't believe we survived." Brandy grimaced and glared out at the sea. Which was hardly fair. It wasn't the sea's fault.

Lily's laugh caught on a gust and danced away. "Of course we survived. It was just a little storm."

"Little?" Brandy tucked a curl behind her ear. "You realize we almost died, right?"

"We didn't almost die—"

"Several times."

"Oh, balderdash."

Brandy studied her with a cynical eye. "You know what your problem is?"

Lily tipped her head to the side. "What?"

"Optimism." A hint of amusement softened the familiar criticism.

"There's nothing wrong with looking on the bright side of things."

"Except that so often, things go to shit. And optimists aren't prepared."

Untrue. Optimists were simply preparing for the best outcome, while pessimists prepared for the worst.

How she and Brandy were friends should have been a mystery. They were so different. But Lily understood. They were friends, and had been since college, *because* they were so different. Each provided a perfect foil for the other.

"Honestly. I know your parents thought they were doing you a favor, sheltering you from the big bad world, but the trouble with that is you have to live in this world, and it's not always lollipops and roses."

Not always. But sometimes.

Still, she couldn't argue with Brandy. Her parents *had* sheltered her. Overprotected her. She'd been cosseted and caged her entire life. Everything had been controlled by her father, or one of his minions—gentlemen in black suits and sunglasses, who spoke to their wrists a lot. She'd never been allowed to do anything wild or crazy. There had been a couple times in college when she'd been able to shake her security team, including one very awkward moment when they'd tracked her down at a kegger and descended like the hounds of hell. Needless to say, she hadn't been invited to many parties after that. But for the most part, she'd never been allowed to do *anything* fun. It had been a point of contention in the family for years.

Now she'd broken away. Now she was living her own life. And it was glorious.

"This trip isn't going to shit," she said. It was an adventure. This opportunity to do something important energized her. Sang in her veins. They were headed to the most exotic place on the planet: Ethiopia. Ethiopia, where they would feed hungry children and rescue puppies and build wells and…make a difference.

"Not going to shit? Are you serious?" Brandy threw out her arms, encompassing the sea. "Do you notice anything missing?"

"Missing?" Lily rumpled her brow.

Brandy sighed. "Were you not paying attention during the orientation?"

Um. No? She'd been preoccupied, thinking about the puppies she could save. Imagining living in a hut for three months and glorying in the freedom of not being *watched* all the time.

It had been such an alluring thought, she'd left without telling anyone—Jeremy, her mother, her father… Daddy was going to have apoplexy when he got the letter telling him where she'd gone. It had been unfair to send a letter, but if she'd told him in person, he would have stopped her.

"Lily…"

"Umm hmm?"

"The convoy? The convoy we're supposed to be a part of until we reach Kenya?"

Lily glanced out at the glassy waters, deep blue and dancing with speckles of sunlight. Beautiful. And yes, empty. A trickle of unease sifted through her. "Where did they go?"

"Where did *we* go is the more pertinent question. We must have gotten separated during the storm. Blown off course." She frowned. "We're probably lost."

"The captain knows how to steer a ship," Lily said, trying not to sound too patronizing. Yes. Lily was an optimist and Brandy was a pessimist, but there was a fine line between pessimism and paranoia. "He'll get us back on course. We can hardly miss Africa. It's quite *large*." This last bit, she whispered in a confidential tone.

Brandy was not in the mood for Lily's quirky humor. But then, she rarely was. "I'm not worried about missing Africa. I'm worried about *where* we are. Alone. In the middle of the Indian Ocean." She sent Lily a meaningful look.

It didn't mean anything. "And?"

"Oh Jesus God, Lily. Don't you watch the news?"

Lily wrinkled her nose. "It's too depressing."

"These waters are notorious for pirate attacks. And here we are. Unprotected."

A shiver walked up her spine. Lily forced a laugh, but even to her own ears, it sounded hollow. "Pirates. Really?" She studied the horizon. Nothing. Nothing but ocean and sky as far as the eye could see. There probably were pirates out there, but the sea was vast. The pirates would never find them.

At least…she hoped.

Lunch was charming. The buffet had been set out on the deck so the passengers could enjoy the beautiful day. It featured a delicious soufflé along with a fruit salad and some cold chicken. Lily enjoyed it immensely. A great part of her enjoyment was reveling in the cool ocean breeze, the kiss of the warm sun, and the amusing banter of the other members of the team.

They were an eclectic group, all young people who felt the need to serve. Michael was a civil engineer, just out of the University of Washington. Since they'd attended the same school, they had a lot to chat about. Nancy was a nurse, like Brandy, so they talked business, which Lily found a little boring since she didn't understand most of the terms they used. She had no idea what a tension pneumothorax was, and from the sound of it, she didn't want to know.

Pierre, the lone Frenchman, was very handsome…and quite a flirt. He tried flirting with Brandy, but that went nowhere—Brandy never had much patience for flirty men—so he turned his attention to Lily.

As a result, lunch was charming…until it was interrupted by a flurry on the deck.

At Captain Garnier's barked command, a hubbub erupted. Lily stilled, her lemonade halfway to her mouth; she stared at the seamen scrambling to their stations and pulling out fire hoses.

Garnier rushed over to their table. "Quickly," he said in his thick accent—Lily had been trying to place it for days. It seemed so rude to ask where he was from. "You must go below. Now."

Brandy bristled with energy. "What is it?"

"We've spotted two crafts. Approaching quickly. It could be nothing, but I must ask you all to vacate the deck."

"Is it pirates?" Brandy was like a dog with a bone.

The soufflé in Lily's belly heaved as she scanned the calm waters.

Garnier frowned. "We don't know. We must follow procedure. Please." He gestured toward the bridge. "Down below. Go. Now. There's a hidden cubby in the storage hold. It should be large enough for all of you." He waved at a crewman. "Enrique will show you where it is."

Pierre leaped to his feet. "Nonsense. I shall stay and fight."

Michael shot a glance around the table. "Guess I should, um, stay and fight too."

"Don't be daft," the captain snapped. "My men are trained. You are not. Now go. And take some food and water."

Lily's pulse surged. "Food and water?"

Garnier threaded anxious fingers through his beard. "We don't know how long this will last. And if they are pirates, and they take the ship, you will be glad for it."

Everyone did as he said, skittering toward the stairs to the hold. All but Pierre. He thrust out his chest and set his chin, and headed for the railing.

Lily gaped at him in shock. If the captain said they should hide, they should probably hide. Perhaps it was foolhardy of her to follow Pierre instead of the others, but she felt the needling urge to convince him to go below. To safety.

"Pierre," she said as she tugged his sleeve. "We need to go."

He waved her away with the slash of a hand. His gaze was trained on the approaching boats. They seemed to fly toward them, skimming the waves, jouncing and soaring over the water. There were four men in each craft, and they all had rifles, though one man had what looked like a grenade launcher.

Lily's heart clenched. Her breath caught.

Pirates.

Dang it. She hated when Brandy was right.

The sailors scuttled about, preparing their hoses to repel the onslaught. As the tiny boats neared, a cry went up and streams of water blasted from the lower deck. The pirates changed course, zipping around the bow of their ship to keep from being swamped. In response, they fired several shots. The sharp retorts echoed, twined with the cries of the sailors.

"Down!" Garnier bellowed. "Get down!"

Several more shots rang out, hitting the hull and the bulwarks with dull, staccato pings. Lily flinched with every one.

All this happened in a matter of seconds, but it felt like minutes, hours, as though time had slowed down. Her pulse thudded in her ears. Something bitter rose in her mouth.

"Please, Pierre!" she wailed.

He shot her a frown, but then grudgingly followed.

They raced across the deck to the hatch that led to the lower decks, keeping low—bullets were whizzing by with alarming rapidity. A bullet slammed into the hatch, burying itself in the steel just above their heads, leaving a smoking hole. Pierre *eeped* and pushed past her. He scampered below, nearly bumping into Brandy as she bounded up the stairs.

As her gaze landed on Lily, she cried, "Where the hell have you been?"

"Collecting Pierre. He wanted to watch."

Brandy caught her arm and dragged her down the stairs. "Heaven protect us from innocents and devils," she muttered.

"What's that supposed to mean?"

"Nothing. What were you thinking? Going after Pierre? You need to take care of your own ass. For pity sake, Lily, those were real bullets out there."

Lily swallowed, but she didn't respond. Her throat was too tight.

"A bullet doesn't care who your father is. Understand? And when bullets are flying, anyone can get shot. Trust me. I've patched up more than one bystander who took a stray."

"Well, I didn't get shot." There had been a close one, but she didn't get shot. "Where are we going?"

"Into the hold." Brandy led her down another set of stairs and another. It seemed to get darker as they descended.

Lily wrinkled her nose. "It smells down here."

Brandy gusted a sigh. "Get used to it, Lil. We could be here for a while. The pirates don't just go away. They stay. They follow you.

They continue attacking until you outrun them or until help comes." She pinned Lily with a dark glower. "We're in real danger here. People die in situations like this. They get taken prisoner. Held as hostages. For years sometimes."

Lily's stomach lurched. "H-held as hostages?"

"Yes."

Oh dear.

If she were taken hostage, someone would, in all likelihood, notify her father.

He was going to be furious.

As they ducked into the small cubby in the bow of the boat, behind a pallet of crates marked "Iodine," an explosion rocked the ship. Lily teetered to the side and stepped on someone's foot. It could have been Michael's, but it was hard to tell, because they were all entwined. There was barely room for her to fit.

"Close the door," Pierre trilled. The panic in his tone was unmistakable. It was probably a good thing he had not stayed above to fight. He wasn't alone in his terror though; the scent of fear gripped them all.

Lily arranged herself on the hard wood floor, hunching in so there was more room for the others. The air was already stale with so many people in such a cramped space. And it was warm. She ignored her discomfort and the sounds of the battle, the thrum of the engine, the muted retorts of rifle fire, calming herself with her familiar mantra. *What would happen, would happen.* It always did. Worrying about it, when one was helpless, was pointless. Best to plan for any contingencies. She drew in a deep, calming breath and started running scenarios in her head.

It would be all right. No doubt Garnier had sent a distress signal and the French fleet—or whoever patrolled these waters—would come and chase the pirates off. All they had to do was hold out until then.

The engine revved then, and the ship sped up. Yes. They could outrun them.

But then an explosion from the stern rocked the boat. Everyone in the cubby gasped at the shudder of steel. A scream of metal reverberated, a harsh clunk, and then the engine fell silent.

"Oh God," Nancy wailed. Her face was drenched in sweat, her expression wild.

"It'll be okay, Nancy." Lily patted her hand.

"No. It won't. Don't you see? They've blown out the propellers. We can't run."

"Someone will save us."

Pierre snorted. "It could take days before help comes. Days."

"We'll be fine."

She could tell the others were annoyed by her pronouncements, but Lily was used to that. Optimism annoyed a lot of people. They glared at her, all but Brandy, who wrapped her arm around Lily's shoulder and tugged her close. "I hope you're right," she whispered. "Dear God, I hope you're right."

They knew when the pirates boarded. The sounds wafted down from the upper decks like eerie wraiths. The yells, the cries, gunfire. Pounding footsteps. Calls in some language Lily did not understand. Laughter.

Everyone stiffened as the invaders swarmed down to the hold. Lily held her breath as they ripped open crates, pillaged the cargo, and chattered about their booty. At least, that was what Lily assumed, since she couldn't understand a word.

She nearly fainted when they left, but only because holding her breath had made her dizzy.

It got quiet then, except for the occasional shouts and mysterious thuds. Lily closed her eyes and rested, but she was too wound up to sleep.

Sometime in the night, they came back and began ransacking the hold, searching…for something. Her heart shot into her throat as she heard footsteps nearing their refuge; it swelled when the door to their hiding place rattled. The cubby locked from the inside, but only by a thin bolt.

A voice rang out. More footsteps echoed.

Another rattle. Harder this time.

Nancy made a peep, an anguished whimper. Pierre muffled the sound with his palm. They all sat as still as they could, as quietly as they could, praying the pirates would give up and go away. The tension sizzling around them was a palpable thing.

And then, with a horrifying groan, the teeth of a crowbar slammed between the door and the frame, and the barrier was wrenched open.

The weak beam of the flashlight was nearly blinding as the pirate shined it over them. When it flickered away from her eyes, making it possible to see, Lily froze. Her pulse leapt. The barrel of a rifle was pointed right at her head.

She glanced up at the pirate's face muted in the shadows. He was a young boy, maybe fifteen, skinny and scarred. His clothes were ratty and hung on his bony frame. His pants were torn and he wore thin flip-flops barely large enough for his feet. There was a tinge of triumph on his face as he stared at them, but Lily saw a hint of fear as well.

"Out. Out," he barked, waving the gun as he backed away. His compatriots, also young, huddled around him, their guns poised.

"Slowly," Brandy said under her breath. "And hold up your hands so they know we don't have weapons."

Lily nodded and eased out of the cubby. Her muscles complained. They'd been locked in one position for hours. As she stood and stretched, she sent a wobbly, reassuring smile to her captors.

They did not smile back.

But then, she didn't expect them to.

They were pirates, after all.

And she was their captive.

CHAPTER TWO

Ryder "Stone" Maddox bent as he passed through the hatch into the war room of the *USS Sierra Nevada*. He grimaced. The rest of the squadron was already assembled, all but his team. *Shit.* That meant he owed the other team leaders a round. Rocco and Buzz smirked.

His team had been on training maneuvers in the Gulf of Aden when they'd gotten the recall notice and had to be flown in. They'd only just arrived.

Lieutenant Harper, the officer in charge, stood at the front of the room. As he waited to start the briefing, he chatted with an officer in full uniform who had his back to the crews.

This mission must be important, if the brass was here.

Of course, all their missions were important, but Stone could tell from the crackling energy, this one was different.

He frowned at his men; they winced and double-timed it into the room. Mason, Tate, Garrett, and Luke had their game faces on. Even Zack looked solemn. Only Drake shot him a grin. But then, Drake would.

The little shit had no concept of decorum. Never had.

At the request of Admiral Birch, Drake had just been assigned to Stone's team. Whether Stone liked it or not, he was saddled with him. Not that Drake wasn't one of the best. He was. But he and Stone had a *history*.

Goddamn it.

Harper glanced up as they took their seats. "Nice of you to join us, gentlemen," he quipped. The officer at his side turned, and Stone stilled. Something nasty curled in his gut. *Fuck a duck*. Brandywine himself, the commander of the entire SEAL team.

Definitely important.

Stone shot a glare at his squad, warning them silently to be on their best behavior.

Most of them already knew. Most of them were familiar with Brandywine. He was a legend. Before his promotion into Command, he'd been a SEAL himself. They'd fucking studied him at the Naval Special Warfare Prep School.

Whatever this was, it was huge for him to be here.

Harper cleared his throat. "Okay, boys. Shall we begin?"

A boisterous *"Hooah!"* rang off the walls.

Harper turned on the overhead and a map of the Indian Ocean came up on screen. "The commander is on a tight schedule and wants to address you personally, but before he does, let's go over the mission specs. This is a hostage rescue."

A groan rumbled through Rocco's team. No doubt they were hoping for orders to find Bin Laden…and kill him again.

Harper frowned at them. "Secure that," he clipped.

Rocco glowered at his team. "Aye, aye, sir."

"A Dutch cruise ship named the *Avonturier*, heading for Kenya, was boarded by pirates. The crew and passengers were taken prisoner…here." He whacked the map with his pointer, smack dab in the middle of the ocean off the coast of Somalia.

Stone shared a look with Mason. His expression said it all. *Another pirate attack. Awesome.* They'd served on several rescue missions before, which was probably why they were here.

Buzz raised his hand. "Excuse me, sir. A cruise ship? In the Indian Ocean…off the coast of Somalia?" His tone made his opinion clear. If they were stupid enough to *cruise* in pirate-infested waters, they got what they deserved.

"The ship was blown off course during a recent storm. They were heading for Kenya carrying supplies for an Ethiopian relief project and…" His gaze danced to Brandywine. "A group of aid workers."

"Missionaries," Buzz muttered.

"According to our intelligence, they are being held here"— another whack—"on an island in the Bajuni Archipelago along the southeast point of Somalia."

Stone frowned. Without thought, his hand shot up. Harper had always encouraged them to ask questions during briefings. He usually waited until the end, but this...

"Maddox?"

"Sir. They're being held on an island?" Usually when the clans took ships, they held them offshore and the hostages remained onboard.

Harper nodded, his features harsh. "Lucky for us, this isn't a typical pirate crew." The bite in his tone did not bode well. "Apparently this crew is not affiliated with any of the known clans. The reason they're not parked off the coast while they work on negotiating ransoms is because these geniuses refused to pay the local militia. After which they were asked, not so politely, to leave.

"Since they brilliantly blew the props in the attack, they had to travel by sail, which slowed them down. After being refused at each port, they landed on this island in the Archipelago and basically invaded, killing any of the native Bajuunis who resisted."

Stone's hand shot up again. "Killing, sir?" Typically pirate crews avoided bloodshed if they could. The clans frowned on it as it was not profitable.

"Right." Harper massaged his temples. "These fellows, apparently, are rebels. Or desperate. They've already broken multiple conventions your typical Somali pirate follows. Our intelligence says..." He glanced at the commander again. "At least one of the passengers and three of the crew are dead. The crew members were killed during the firefight and the passenger apparently attempted an escape."

"How many hostages are there?" Rocco asked.

"Twenty-seven crew members and four passengers. From what we can tell, a total of sixteen pirates. There were originally eight, but when they landed on the island, they were joined by another crew." Harper flicked a switch on the remote and a new map came up with the layout of the island. It was long and slender and the topography was fairly flat, but then most archipelagos were little more than glorified reefs. There was a village on each end and an X on the eastern shore, about midpoint, marked as the extraction point. "We believe the pirates are holding the hostages here." He pointed to the village on the south end of the island. "Squads three, four, and five, this is your target. Your mission...take out the pirates and rescue those hostages.

"Squad two, you clear and hold the landing zone here. We'll send Chinooks out for pickup when you radio in. Squad one, you're tasked with clearing the village to the north. According to our drones, there's not much activity there, but some hostiles have been spotted in the vicinity."

Stone nodded, swallowing his disappointment. He'd hoped to be part of the frontal assault. Every SEAL wanted to be in the middle of the action pretty much all the time, but he knew each task was critical to the overall mission or it wouldn't be a task. Clearing and securing the northern village would protect the troops at the extraction point as well as the ones working to the south.

But damn.

Harper scanned the company with a razor-sharp gaze. "Our top priority is the four passengers."

"Wait," Buzz piped up. "The four passengers?"

He shouldn't have piped up.

Harper gored him with a glare.

"These are high-profile passengers." Every head whipped to Brandywine who, until now, had not spoken.

"High profile, sir?" Something tensed in Stone's gut. *Crap*. He hated anything high profile.

The commander nodded to Harper, who switched the screen. An angel appeared. No. Not an angel. A girl. A woman. Ethereal, beautiful with soft blonde hair and sparkling blue eyes. The lines of her face were delicate and perfectly symmetrical. Even her teeth were straight. She held a puppy in her arms and smiled with a brilliance that should have blinded him.

Whistles rounded the room. Harper didn't even bother to glare everyone down.

Goddamn, she was gorgeous.

Stone's lust rose and he wrangled it back.

This was a briefing. She was a target. A high-profile target. The worst possible kind. There was no room for lust in his work. When the thought occurred that he probably needed to get laid, he pushed that away too.

He focused instead on the delicate features, the vulnerability in her eyes. *Shit*. A woman like this, in the hands of heartless pirates? The thought tore at him, and his resolve to do what he could to bring her home unharmed swelled.

"This, gentlemen, is Liliana Wilson." Harper shot a hard look at each and every man. "What? Name not familiar to you?"

"No, sir." A chorus.

"Maybe you've heard of her father? Senator Oberon Wilson?"

Silence settled on the assemblage.

Shitfuck.

A senator.

They were the worst.

And Wilson was the front-runner for the vice presidential slot in the next election. Could this get any worse?

"The other passengers..." Harper shuffled through the papers on his clipboard. "Pierre LeMarc, a French sociology student. Michael Tippet, an engineer. Nancy Sayers, a nurse and..." He glanced at the commander and toggled to the next slide. Another smiling girl. This one with auburn pigtails, a raft of freckles over her nose, a crooked smile...and braces. "Susan Brandywine."

All eyes snapped to the commander. All but Drake's. "Shit," he muttered. "Is she seven?"

Brandywine's expression tightened as he stared at the picture of the little girl. *His* little girl. When he spoke, his voice was rough. "This is the only photo I have of her. The last one her mother sent me. She is...older now." His throat worked. "If you boys could bring my daughter home safely, I would be very appreciative."

"Yes, sir." The response was automatic. As though there was any possibility of failure. They were Navy SEALs for fuck sake. They never failed.

The commander nodded and checked his watch. Then, after a whispered confab with Harper, he sketched a salute to the men and left the room. When the door closed behind him, a ruckus broke out.

Harper silenced them all with a wave of his hand. "I didn't want to stress this in front of him, but you all need to be aware. This is not your typical pirate crew. For most of these bastards, this is just a business. The crews try very hard to keep their hostages safe and in good health. They are respectful of women. These guys... Well, they've already killed one hostage that we know of."

Stone's attention tracked back to the picture of Susan Brandywine. He set his teeth as he thought of what could have happened to her, what could be happening now.

"Needless to say, time is of the essence. Team medics, be sure your bags are stocked. We have no idea what we'll find." Harper scrolled back to the slide showing the map of the island. Though it only flickered for a second as he toggled through, that vision of the angel hit Stone like a fist to the gut. Again.

"Okay. Here's how it's going to play out. It will be a nighttime incursion. We'll be flying you in with a HAHO drop out of Lemonnier." Not a surprise. If one wanted to be stealthy, a High Altitude High Opening was the best way to infiltrate a target, and Lemonnier was the closest airfield that could handle a C-17. That they were dropping in over the Indian Ocean, shooting for a tiny island, wasn't a concern. With their gear and Mason's navigation skills, they could land on a dime.

At Stone's side, Drake gave a little chuckle. He loved nighttime drops—probably because jumping out of an airplane from a high altitude in the pitch dark was one of the most dangerous maneuvers they did. And Drake loved a thrill. He always had.

"We're doing concurrent drops with the first team to the north." Harper glanced at Stone. "The second team to the extraction point and the other teams to the south. Try not to tangle. Assault teams, once you land, clear the villages, collect your hostages, and make your way here, to the east coast at the center of the island for extraction. We'll have choppers standing by on this carrier just out of line of sight." He blew out a breath and his gaze rounded the room. "Any questions?"

"Yes, sir." Buzz offered a snarky grin. "What if the mission goes tits up?"

Harper was not amused. But then, he rarely was. He was a damn good leader but took no shit off anyone. "Your first priority is those hostages. Whatever it takes to get them out."

"And the secondary extraction point?" Stone asked. He had to ask. More than once, he'd needed one. Shit happened in the field. Shit happened a lot.

"If, for some reason, you can't make it to the eastern shore, head for this promontory on the southern coast. At low tide, you can wade across to the next island, but watch your timing or you could be swimming."

Buzz snorted. Harper narrowed his eyes. "Yes, I know you boys can swim with sixty-pound packs, but we don't know if your hostages can. And if the tide is coming in, the current could be strong. Not to mention the sand sharks. Your best bet…don't need the secondary extraction point. Okay. Everybody good?"

"Aye aye, sir!"

"Good. Keep your ears on and your coms open. Anything else?" He scanned the assembly. "Nothing? Okay. We'll deploy in two hours. Mess is still open," he said with a wan grin. "Today's special is Shit on a Shingle." A groan rose. "Eat up, boys. For the next few days, it's MREs. Dismissed."

A rustle of activity rose as the SEALs all collected their gear and filed from the room. Drake gusted a laugh as he stood. He laced his fingers and cracked his knuckles. Stone had always hated that. Ever since they'd been kids. His grin was annoying too. "What do ya say, Ryder?" he chirped. "Pretty fucking exciting, isn't it? Our first mission together and we get to rescue a senator's daughter?"

Stone frowned. "Just don't get your ass killed," he muttered.

"Hey, I'm hardly a bubblegummer." Drake smirked. "I did earn the Silver Star, you know."

Hell yeah, he knew. Drake never let him forget it. Brought it up every chance he got. He'd graduated boot camp in a Hall of Fame company—perfect marks—and since he'd earned his trident, he'd been on one award-winning mission after another—including the one where he saved an admiral and his entire entourage.

It would be hell having him on the team because, damn it all, Drake was like a brother to him. Though all the guys on his team were like brothers, Stone managed to keep some emotional distance when it came to the missions. With Drake, it was going to be tough.

They'd grown up together. Their families were close. When they were younger, Drake had followed Stone around like a puppy dog. He'd joined the SEALs because Stone had. Drake's mom still held him responsible for that.

If anything happened to Drake under Stone's watch, Elaine would kill him. And then his own mom would kill him again.

CHAPTER THREE

Excitement whipped through Stone as the C-17 fired up and lifted into the sky. The teams were seated in the belly of the plane in the order they would drop. His team was closest to the ramp, because they'd be jumping first.

His head was a little light—from the excitement, sure, but probably because his system was flooded with O2. As always, they'd done an hour of prep with oxygen, getting their bodies ready for the high-altitude jump, and while each man had a special HAHO helmet, equipped with oxygen, the prep was necessary.

Stone and Mason shared a grin. As nervous as they were, this was exhilarating. It always was. Every time. "Check your gear, guys," he barked through his mic. Though they'd checked it and checked it again, another pass never hurt.

A metallic clatter rumbled through the cabin as his men reviewed their weapons, their ammo, and their packs. "Checks five-oh," they all responded.

Excellent.

Stone went through his gear as well, paying special attention to his main weapon, a suppressed HK416 with an infrared laser, magnifier, and a Nightforce scope. It was his favorite because it was fucking sweet.

Each man on his team carried multiple weapons, and each had his favorite. Tate preferred his M4 assault rifle and Mason had the SAW—the Squad Automatic Weapon. Garrett and Luke both fought over the pirate gun, a blunt-nosed M79 grenade launcher, and of course they each carried a SIG Sauer P226.

Drake just liked them all. And it didn't matter which he carried; he was lethal with anything. Even a KA-BAR.

He leaned around Mason and shot Stone a grin. "Hey, Ryder—" he began, but Mason cut him off with a smack to the back of his head.

"You gotta call him *Stone*, doofus."

"What?" Drake snorted.

Zack nodded. "Ya do…if you're gonna be in this platoon, son."

Garrett and Luke—the Zipperhead Twins, so called because they were nearly identical, right down to their hideous haircuts—chimed in with, "Damn straight."

Drake put out a lip. "How come *I* don't have a nickname?"

"I thought he had one," Tate said, glancing around the cabin, a shit-eating grin on his face.

"Yeah. It's Doofus." Zack snickered.

"A real nickname. And not something lame, like Raven or Hawk."

Luke and Garrett—Raven and Hawk—bristled.

"You don't just *get* a nickname," Mason explained. All the guys guffawed at his patronizing tone. "You have to *earn* it."

"What do I have to do to earn one?"

Stone glowered at him. "Survive," he barked. "Fucking survive this mission." He turned away. He had enough on his mind without worrying about a nickname for Drake. Although Doofus was definitely a contender.

The six-minute call came, and with it, the ramp of the C-17 opened up like a gaping maw. Stone peered out at the night, though there was nothing to see. It was dark; the sky was cloudy. Not even a moon tonight. The wind was cooperating. Perfect for a raid, although once they landed, things could get dicey.

They'd all done hundreds of precision drops before. The standard operating procedure was to touch down away from the target, and then patrol in. This was supposed to be a surprise attack in the middle of the night. He could only hope the stillness didn't work against them. They were coming in high enough that the pirates wouldn't hear the approaching engines, but so much as a stray breeze could give them away when they got close to the island.

At the three-minute warning, all the men came to attention. The jumpmaster signaled them to don their helmets and check their oxygen, waiting for each man to respond that they were good to go. He raised his arm, cuing the teams to stand and prepare for the jump. Mason took the lead, stopping at the hinge of the ramp. Stone went last. He would float on the top of the stack, watching each man's strobe to make sure they lined up correctly.

The jump light flashed green and Stone's pulse kicked up a notch. God, he loved this.

In a well-practiced formation, his team stepped out, man by man, into the open air.

As always, it was a rush, free falling, wind whipping at his face, the drone of the engines replaced by the whistle in his ears. Stone's drogue chute popped off, stabilizing him. He did his checks as he watched the chutes below him plume out, right on cue. Like a well-oiled machine, they formed a perfect stack. Damn, his guys were good.

He yanked the handle, opening his main chute. The canopy released in a billowing ripple. It caught with a snap. The silence of pure sky surrounded him—his favorite part of the jump.

As they neared the target, Stone could make out the shapes of the little islands growing larger. Mason veered to the one he recognized from the sat photo and the team followed. As they drifted toward the north shore, Stone scanned the area. To the south, the parachutes of the other teams silently blossomed. He turned his attention to their target, the northern village. A fire in the middle of a huddle of huts glowed green through the scope of his night-vision goggles.

Stone flared out his chute and landed in the soft sand. They all touched down on the beach, all but Zack, who splashed down in the water. Stone tried not to frown. It was a small mistake in the scheme of things, but one small mistake could get them all killed.

Without a word, they stripped off their harnesses, bundled up their chutes, and switched from jump to assault gear. They headed out in standard formation along the beach, weapons up, locked, and loaded. When the tiny village came into view, Stone held up his fist and his team halted. Everyone took a knee as Garrett scanned the scene with a thermal scope. He drew pictures in the sand of the layout so everyone understood what was what. If they needed to talk, they whispered into the coms. When his crackled, Stone thumped it with a finger until the static cleared.

He had two buds in. The one in his right ear was the troop net, where he and his guys communicated. In his left ear, he heard updates from Command on the status of the overall mission.

They all wore a brand-spanking-new version of the bone phone the quartermaster had issued, and while they had trained with it—their motto was "train like you fight"—this was their first mission with the new equipment. So far, Stone was not impressed. The feed in his left ear cut out and he tapped it again until it picked back up.

The other teams had all deployed. As soon as they were in position, the Head Shed would give the order to go.

In the meantime, they continued their recon. Based on the heat signatures in the village, there was one warm body in each of the four huts. Though based on the intel, they didn't expect to find hostages, they had to go in prepared for anything. The glowing huddle around the fire was definitely pirates. Stone counted three of them. Mason surveyed the scene through his 3x scope and identified that they all had AK-47s…which lay beside them on the ground.

Piece of cake.

The real challenge would be securing the unknown threats in the huts. Garrett would clear the first hut, Luke the second, Drake the third, and Stone would take the fourth. Zack and Tate would neutralize the pirates by the fire while Mason, with the SAW, would provide cover if needed. Their mission was to disarm and confine the hostiles and make sure there were no hostages being held here. If there were, their mission would shift to rescue, to get the hostages to the extraction point as quickly as possible.

Regardless, they needed to clear the village.

Protocol allowed the use of deadly force only if the team or the hostages were in danger, but his men knew how to take a man down without killing him.

They knew how to kill a man too.

Naturally they preferred the nonlethal method of dealing with a hostile. The alternative involved too much paperwork.

Intel had guestimated sixteen pirates on the island. That meant there were more out there somewhere, though they were probably concentrated on the south end. If the pirates knew what they were doing, they would have some men out on patrol as well.

When the *go* signal came through on the Command net, Stone motioned to his men and they melted into the shadows. He quickly followed. They had trained for missions like this, and then trained some more. They all knew their roles and while they had their ears on, there was little need for chatter. As a man, they moved with deathly silence.

The huts were in a U-shaped formation, so he could see his men approach their targets. With the exception of the murmuring pirates huddled around the fire, the village was deserted and silent. Stone held his weapon at the ready as he scanned the area around his target hut. He edged around the back then slowly slipped into position.

"Chipmunk one, set." Garrett's low voice crackled through his earpiece.

Really? They were going with the Chipmunks?

There was a thread of laughter in Luke's response. "Chipmunk two, set."

"Chipmunk three, set," Drake said in a clipped tone. For all he was a dipwad, he could be serious when he needed to be.

Stone tried very hard to keep a straight face as he whispered, "Chipmunk four, set."

He could hear the smile in Mason's voice as he gave his ready call. "Dave, set."

Seriously. The guys really needed to quit watching cartoons.

Zack and Tate eased into position behind the guards and, at a motion from Mason, lunged.

It was over in seconds. The pirates were little more than boys. Too inexperienced to even have their rifles close at hand. With practiced flair, Garrett quickly gagged them and secured them with flex cuffs. Once they were incapacitated, Mason motioned to the rest of the team to move in. Stone used the barrel of his rifle to ease open the flap covering the door of his hut. While their recon had shown there was a warm body in each hut, they were probably pirates, so extreme caution was necessary.

He leaned in for a quick scan…and froze.

The hovel was dark, but in the green haze of his night-vision goggles, he saw her face.

His breath caught. *The angel.*

Liliana Wilson.

She was sleeping. Her sooty lashes arched over her cheeks. Her lips were parted. Soft skeins of gossamer hair curled around her shoulders. Her alabaster skin glowed. Her tongue peeped out as she grunted in her sleep. The exquisite lines of her face were marred only by a dark bruise on her chin.

The sight of her dazzled him.

But he couldn't afford to be dazzled.

"I have a target," he said softly. "Repeat. I have a target."

"Roger that," Drake replied. "I have a target too."

Garrett and Luke gave the same response. *Shit.* What were the odds they would hit the lottery? That all four of the passengers were being held in their village?

"Team one has four targets," he told Command. "Shifting to plan B." Their top priority now was to get these hostages to safety.

He slipped through the door, hunkered down, and set his hand on her shoulder. Her eyes fluttered open and her gaze hit him like a grenade blast. *Holy hell.* Wide and clear. She was even more stunning in person. And warm. She was warm.

He pointed to his call sign patch, which identified him as one of the good guys, though it was clear from her expression she knew just who he was.

Her mouth opened—fascinating, that—and he put a finger to her lips.

Though they had dispatched the guards, there was no telling if more were around. They had to assume there were. Best to remain as quiet as possible.

Still, he couldn't stop the groan that escaped him when she smiled. Because, holy God, it was a hellish smile. Impish and crooked and far too appealing. Her soft lips moved against his finger in a tantalizing brush. Despite himself, he was tempted to yank her into his arms and kiss her.

Where such a notion came from, he had no clue.

Brutally, he shoved his inconvenient lust away. He could think about it later, when they were all safe. He took her arm with a bit too much force. She flinched.

"Sorry," he murmured, though to his ears, he didn't sound sorry in the slightest. He reminded himself not to care, to focus on his primary objective: getting her safe. He peered out of the hut and checked the clearing.

Zack, Mason, and Tate were holding their ground by the fire, scanning the area, ready to provide cover for their retreat if needed. Garrett and Luke had their hostages in tow and were heading back to the beach. But of Drake there was no sign. Stone's gut clenched. He should be out by now. Where the hell was he?

He was about to utter the incongruous words "Chipmunk three" when he saw him. The breath gushed out of Stone as Drake emerged from the hut, supporting a limping woman.

Stone gave the signal for retreat; his men by the fire began backing toward the huts.

"I've got movers," Mason clipped, just before a shout rang out from beyond the clearing.

Shit.

Four shadows danced along the tree line and hunkered behind an outcropping.

Steeling himself, Stone lifted his weapon, shoving his hostage behind him in the same motion.

The *pop pop pop* of gunfire hailed them. Lights flared from the enemy's position as the chatter of AK-47 fire peppered the dirt of the encampment. Mason returned fire as Zack and Tate edged back. The SAW went hot, spraying the rocks with hundreds of rounds.

More shouts…and then all hell broke loose.

Rifle shots and blasts from automatic weapons raked the little village. The guys by the fire dove for cover. One of the pirates stood, holding an RPG. He fired. Stone saw it coming in, screaming directly toward his position, and instinctively hunched his body over the tiny woman by his side. The grenade hit the hut and it exploded in a rain of fire and debris. Something heavy hit his shoulder but he shook it off.

Even though they were pinned down, his men continued to return fire.

From the corner of his eye, Stone saw Drake push his hostage toward the beach. His buddy stumbled as a round hit him in the leg, but he didn't stop. Another slammed into his back and he pitched forward, propelled by the force of it.

Stone calmed his breathing. They all wore heavy packs and body armor. Drake was fine. Indeed, he kept going despite a pronounced hobble. He disappeared into the scrub surrounding the camp.

To cover Drake's retreat, Stone laid down suppressive fire, aiming for the bursts of light from the AK-47s. He heard a wail and then silence.

The men all held position, scanning for movement. Then Zack tacked to the right, circling around to clear the area behind the rocks.

To Stone's horror, a shadow rose and spattered his buddy with a flurry of bullets; he jerked with each one. With his body armor, he could have survived...if one of the rounds hadn't hit him right between the eyes. It slammed into him with a force that blew his helmet off. There was no doubt. Zack was gone.

Stone was trained for this. He'd seen men die. But the shock was always there.

"Eagle down," he whispered into his mic. There was no response. He tapped it and tried again. Nothing. Not even static.

Shit. The debris from the blast must have knocked out his coms.

His fingers tightened of their own accord and he railed back with a rain of fire, giving Mason time to scuttle for cover, dragging Zack's limp form behind him.

Another shadow rose. With a snarl, Stone aimed and fired and scored another hit. Tate fired as well, catching yet another before following the others.

With one last glance at the clearing, Stone turned and scooped up his hostage and ran for the beach. They had to move fast because if they hadn't neutralized them all, the pirates would follow, so he carried her. Judging from her squirming and mutters, she didn't care for the treatment. She was a tiny thing. He hardly noticed her weight. Her warmth, though, her softness, he noticed.

When they reached the sand, he set her on her feet. "Come on," he said. "Run."

Hunkering low, they made their way along the shore, using the cover of the undergrowth to hide their movements. His coms were totally dead and he couldn't see any of his men. Luke and Garrett had gone ahead with Drake and their hostages, but Tate and Mason would be bringing up the rear, one of them carrying out Zack's body because SEALs never left a man behind.

Even though he couldn't communicate and even though he had no idea where anyone else was, Stone knew he had one mission. Saving the senator's daughter. He had to get to that landing zone and get her on the evac chopper. And once she was safe, he could go back for his men...if they didn't show up.

He stilled as a sharp call echoed off to his right.

Goddamn it. The pirates had cut around through the brush and were coming up behind them. Close. Too close.

A shot whizzed over his head.

Liliana made an *eep* and bent lower.

Stone herded her closer to the tree line. They dodged bushes as they moved inland. If they followed the coastline they would find the LZ and, hopefully, his men would be there.

Another burst of shots rang out. They pinged off the rocks that littered the dark landscape.

Something hit him in the back of the head below the rim of his helmet, and hit him hard. The strap snapped and his helmet tipped off. A sharp pain screamed through his skull.

He tried to keep moving, but his vision blurred. His knees went limp. Still, he pushed on.

Get her safe. Get her safe. It was the only thought in his spinning head.

But then, just like a stone, he fell.

"Oh dear," came a soft gasp from the woman he was supposed to be saving. It was the last thing he heard before everything went black.

"Mister? Mister?"

Lily shook her savior, but to no avail. Oh, she did so hope he wasn't dead. She'd always thought herself a laid-back kind of person, with a "What will be, will be" attitude. But at the moment, she didn't feel so blasé. He wasn't moving, this mountain of a man, and she *needed* him. Fear coiled in her chest. She stared at him, willing her eyes to focus through the murk. With great relief she saw his chest rise.

Thank God. He wasn't dead. But…

A rustle in the distance and a random shot reminded her that even though they'd moved inland and were somewhat cloaked by the scrub, they were hardly safe. If the pirates came past this spot, they *would* see them. Her hair alone was like a beacon.

She could easily run. She could probably hide successfully, but she couldn't leave *him*. She gazed down at her rescuer. In the shadows, she couldn't make out any of his features. But what she did know was he had a low, melodious and very reassuring voice. And he weighed a ton. Probably an actual ton.

When he'd fallen, the earth had trembled.

And he had saved her.

Maybe.

Probably.

It was only polite to save him back.

Another call, closer, sent her hurtling into action. She fumbled about her rescuer's belt until she found something that felt like the hilt of a knife. She pulled it from its scabbard with a deadly ring. It glinted with what little light there was. A shudder rippled through her.

Holy Hannah. *This* was a knife.

Without hesitation she cut several bushes and laid them over him. She had to bend his legs up so his long body would be off the path, but she was able to manage that. Then she covered her head with the "modesty shawl" the pirates had given her, and hunkered down by his side...just as a group of scruffy men came into view.

Lily froze as she recognized them. Kaafi, Mahdi, and Saalim.

Mahdi and Saalim weren't so bad, but Kaafi had cuffed her so hard the first day here, she'd tumbled to the ground. And he'd *looked* at her. With a very unpleasant glint in his eyes. She sucked in a breath and held it as they walked by, guns raised, scanning the beach. A bug crawled on her cheek. She didn't even stir to wave it away.

Just as they passed, her rescuer groaned. Lily's heart lurched. She clapped her hand over his mouth. Kaafi stopped and glanced around with narrowed eyes. Lily counted the seconds in the throb of her pulse.

When he finally turned and followed the others, she nearly collapsed, but she didn't. She was too frightened to move.

She sat in that position, without so much as a twitch, for a very long time. The familiar sounds of the night enrobed her. She listened to the shush of waves, the occasional caw of a night bird, the chirp of crickets, trying to hear above it all. And, for God's sake, trying not to fall sleep.

A dull thudding sound snapped her to attention. She scanned the sky and saw several long, narrow shadows approach. Her heart lifted, and then it dropped like a lead weight. Even if she leaped to her feet and screamed and waved her arms, the helicopters would never see her.

But she might attract a pirate or two.

So instead of running out onto the beach as she longed to do, she hunkered deeper and watched the choppers pass them by.

Her choice was a good one. For even as the choppers disappeared from view, she heard a cry go up behind her and the pounding footsteps as the pirates raced to intercept the crafts.

Thankfully, they were running *away* from her flimsy shelter.

The night wore on and Lily remained as vigilant as she could, guarding her savior. Occasionally she checked his neck for a pulse and was reassured when she found it; it seemed stronger each time. That simple touch was more heartening than she ever could have imagined. Beyond that, his neck was smooth, his skin soft and warm. She found herself resting her hand there, even when she wasn't checking for a pulse, just so she didn't feel so alone.

She wondered about him. What his name was. How badly he was hurt. What his life was like… She decided it must be very exciting indeed, if this was a typical night for him. She'd often wished she were a daring soul. Wished she could have wild, madcap adventures.

Although, after this, she would probably pass on adventures for a while.

In retrospect, she realized it had been wrong of her to sneak off with Brandy on this trip without telling anyone—her family must be worried sick—but she'd desperately needed to get away…and live for once. If she married Jeremy, as her parents wanted, this would be the last thing she ever did that was in the slightest spontaneous. Or daring. Or interesting.

She brushed away a bug and wrinkled her nose. She didn't want to marry Jeremy.

Not that there was anything wrong with him. He didn't smell bad or yell at her. He brought her chocolates—though not the ones she liked. He had a Jaguar. And a beach house. And a hot tub.

But these weren't what she wanted in a marriage. She wanted a soul mate, someone she could talk to and laugh with. She wanted that one great love. She wanted…passion.

And while Jeremy had passion—for his Jag, for his beach house, and even for her, when football wasn't on—she'd discovered *she* didn't have passion for *him*. At least, not the kind of passion she longed for.

She'd never met a man who made her feel the way she wanted to feel, but she knew there had to be more. Some elusive…something. She'd just never found it in any of the men she'd dated. She wasn't sure if it was their fault, her fault, or just nobody's fault.

The more she thought about it, the more she realized she probably didn't want to get married at all. If nothing else, this trauma had made one thing crystal clear.

This was *her* life. The only one she got—unless the Hindus were right and there was such a thing as reincarnation. But that was hardly the point. The point was, *she* was in charge.

Maybe her life had been so boring because she'd let her father script it. Maybe it was time to grab hold of the reins, whether he liked it or not. And even though this rebellion hadn't worked out so well, perhaps the next one would.

The man at her side groaned again and Lily stroked his hair. She had no idea where his helmet had gone. He'd lost it sometime during their headlong flight, or when he'd fallen, but she didn't want to leave him to look for it. Her fingers came across a damp spot on the back of his head, most likely where he'd been hit. It didn't feel like a bullet wound—not that she knew what one might feel like. At any rate, there wasn't much she could do about it in the dark.

She felt carefully for any other injuries and when she found none, she relaxed and curled up by his side and used him as her pillow.

Hopefully he wouldn't mind.

In the end, she didn't care if he did mind, because he was a terrible pillow. He was, in fact, as hard as a rock.

CHAPTER FOUR

Stone opened his eyes and winced as the sunlight scored his corneas. Then he groaned as that tiny wince sent a shard of pain through his head. He tried to sit up but something was weighing him down. *What the—*

He glanced at his chest and froze. A tangle of feathery curls spread out all over his body. *She* was spread out all over his body. And shit, it felt good.

The events of the previous night washed through him and he almost winced again; he stopped himself in time.

What a clusterfuck.

The mission had gone bad and in a big way.

He had no idea if his men had reached the LZ with their hostages. No idea if they were dead or alive. If they'd been taken prisoner.

He had no idea if Drake was safe.

Shit.

It didn't matter though. He couldn't afford to go back and check. The pirates were still out there, and heavily armed. What he did know was that they'd missed the pick-up. His best option was to continue to the secondary extraction point on the other island. Without moving, he checked the angle of the sun—early morning—and calculated the direction they needed to head.

It would be dangerous moving during the day—the pirates had probably increased their patrols—but if they kept to the tree line, making sure to walk on the packed dirt, they wouldn't leave a trail.

He looked down at her again and his heart swelled. Damn, she was a pretty thing. Especially asleep. Her features were soft and sweet, her mouth slightly agape. A tiny snore rumbled. He hated to wake her, but they needed to get moving.

"Liliana?" He shook her gently. "Liliana?"

She snuffled and murmured—again, fascinating to watch those lips move—and then her eyes opened. As it had last night in the shadows of the hut, her gaze gutted him. Bright and blue, clear. Her lashes fluttered. They were long and dark, a stunning counterpoint to her light hair.

She stared at him for a moment. "Oh," she said. "Hello."

He attempted a smile. "Good morning."

Her mouth worked as though she was searching for words. Then she said the most incongruous thing. "I'm so glad you are not dead."

He couldn't stop his bark of laughter. He wished he had, because it hurt. "I'm glad too."

She sat up and he tried to ignore the wave of regret as she angled away, out from under the bushes that shielded them. Had he really thought to hold her…forever? She brushed her tangled hair from her face and stared at him with wide eyes. "I wasn't sure for a while."

"I'm fine." He tried to follow her out of the foliage, but it clung to him. He realized it wasn't rooted to the ground. "What is this?" he muttered, pushing it away.

"Oh. They were coming, so I borrowed your knife and cut some branches for us to hide under." She blinked as his attention snapped to her. "I…hope you don't mind."

Mind?

She wrinkled her nose and gestured to his waist. "I put it back."

Holy hell. "*They* were coming, so you cut a bunch of branches and covered us?"

"Y-yes. They would have found us if I hadn't."

No doubt.

Shit. He benched twice her weight on a typical day, and she—this tiny thing—had saved his life. Cut some bushes to hide them. In the dark. Under extreme pressure.

He realized he was staring at her, probably the way he stared at his men sometimes, because her chin wobbled. "I put it back," she repeated in a small voice.

He forced a smile, because it seemed necessary to reassure her. And, perhaps, because he felt like smiling. "Sweetheart, you saved us both. Are you sure you're not a SEAL?"

And damn, it was worth it, that smile, when relief flooded her features and she grinned back. He had no idea why his heart skipped a beat. You would have thought he'd hung the moon, the way she gazed at him. But all she said was, "Oh. Good. I'm Lily, by the way." She thrust out her hand.

He was loath to take it, but did. Tingles danced up his arm. "Stone." Her snort surprised him. "What?"

"Nothing." Her eyes glimmered. It wasn't nothing. "Is that your real name?"

"It's what people call me."

"Why do they call you Stone?"

He lifted a shoulder. "Because I'm hard." Hard-hearted. Cold as a stone. Impervious. But he didn't feel cold around her. Around her, he felt hot.

She nodded. "You are hard. I noticed that last night."

His pulse leaped. Something tightened at his core.

"Not a very good pillow at all."

Oh. Right. *That* kind of hard.

"It's probably all my gear," he said gruffly, patting his vest, which was filled with ballistic plates, ordnance, survival gear, and all kinds of shit. And she'd slept on him. Draped over him—

His cock stirred. He raked his hair and cringed when he hit a tender spot on the back of his scalp. His hand came back bloody.

She gasped. "Oh, we should probably tend that."

He nodded and pulled out his small first aid kit. An alcohol swab was probably as good as it got for now. To his horror, she took it from him and walked on her knees behind him.

"Oh my," she murmured as she studied his wound, riffling her fingers through the stubble of his hair. He flinched when she touched him. "Did that hurt?"

Not in the way she meant. "It's fine. Just swab it and make sure it's clean, okay?"

"Okay." Her touch was gentle. She dabbed at the wound tentatively. He would have just burrowed in. "I think it was a piece of rock," she said. "I was worried it was a bullet."

"It wasn't a bullet." He knew what a bullet felt like. "Most likely a ricochet."

"That's what I was thinking. Should I wrap it?"

He frowned over his shoulder at her. Right. Just what he needed, to stumble across the island looking like the walking dead. "No. It'll be fine." He pulled away, because she was still stroking his scalp and it was far too alluring. No. Not alluring. Annoying. That's what it was. "Thank you. Have you, um, seen my helmet?" If he lost it, he'd never live it down. The night-vision goggles alone were worth a fortune.

"Let me look." She stood slowly, scanning the area, checking for hostiles, before she made her way through the grasses and scrub, hunting for his brain bucket. He would have helped, but his head was still a little woozy; he focused on getting his vision to uncross. "I don't see it," she huffed, dropping back down by his side.

Stone nodded. When he found his feet, he'd search as well. It had to be here. "Are you hungry?"

He asked because her belly growled loudly enough to attract pirates on the mainland.

"A little." She licked her lips. "But I'm really thirsty."

He pulled out the straw of his CamelBak and leaned forward, holding it to her lips. He should have shuttled off all his gear and just handed the damn thing to her, because when she leaned in close and he got a whiff of her, he nearly passed out. You would think a woman who had been held prisoner by filthy pirates for nearly a week would smell bad. She did not. She smelled like heaven. There was a light musky odor of sweat—it was hot in the tropics—but it twined with something that was essentially female.

He'd never felt such hunger. It screamed through his soul.

And, on top of that, their faces were close. And she was sucking on the nozzle. And *fuck*.

He was a warrior. A trained weapon. On a mission.

This was no time for a hard-on.

But he was hard. Damn hard.

Her lashes flickered as she glanced up at him; she moaned as she swallowed. A shiver walked down his spine. Walked right down his spine and coiled in his balls.

When she sat back with a sigh, he put the nozzle to his lips as well. Not because he was particularly thirsty, but because he wanted a taste of her mouth, while it was still fresh.

What he really wanted was to kiss her. But she was the senator's daughter and he was a grunt. That wasn't going to happen. It couldn't.

"Did…did you say something about food?" Damn lashes. Fluttering again. He had the urge to grab his Gerber and snip them off.

He pulled an MRE from a pocket on his left leg, read the label, and grimaced. He hated the meatloaf. He should have paid more attention when he prepped his gear. He had more in his pack, but this would do for now. "I have this."

Her nose wrinkled as she studied the silver foil.

Yeah. Wait 'til she got a taste. He ripped open the packet, broke off a piece, and handed it to her. It was messy because of the gravy, but he didn't want to unload everything to find an implement. They needed to eat and go.

She took a bite. Her eyes widened. "Yuuum," she said in an unconvincing tone.

It was all he could do to hold back his laugh.

"What…" She swallowed heavily. "What is this?"

"An MRE."

"What does that stand for?"

His lips quirked. "Meals Rarely Edible."

Her brow wrinkled, and then she laughed.

And ah, what a laugh. A melodic trill. Some kind of sound he figured you might hear in heaven.

"Do you eat these often?"

"Not if I can help it." He shoved a chunk in his mouth and fired it back. "But we have a long way to go today, and these have a lot of calories."

She froze, a niblette of mystery meat halfway to her mouth. "H-how many calories?"

"About twelve hundred a meal."

She gaped at him. "Twelve *hundred*?" She glared at the meatloaf as though it were made of turds. Then again, it might have been. "And you gave it to me? To eat?"

"Yeah. You'll need it."

"Why didn't you warn me?" She smacked him. It was like being batted by a kitten. "Twelve hundred calories is my whole day!"

He grinned. He could burn that much with a good fart. "Perfect. It's probably all you'll get. Eat up."

"For twelve hundred calories, I could have eaten a cheesecake."

He looked around for the cheesecake.

She shoved her tiny chunk of meatloaf at him. "Here, you eat it."

He pushed it back. "You eat it. We have a lot of ground to cover today."

"We do?" She tipped her head to the side. "Where are we going?"

"There's an island to the south." He grabbed a stick and sketched out a quick map. "We're here. At the north end of this island. And the secondary extraction point is here."

Her throat worked. "How will we get to the other island?"

"Swim."

She paled. "I-I can't swim."

It was probably rude to stare. But really? She couldn't swim? Who couldn't swim? "You never wanted to learn?"

"Oh, I wanted to." She sighed. "My mother was afraid I would drown."

"Not drowning is kind of the point of swimming."

"She wanted to keep me safe." He didn't miss the exasperation in her tone. "I didn't get to do a lot of things. Which is probably why— And wouldn't you know it? The first time?" She gazed at him as though she'd finished a sentence. As though he'd understood a bit of what she'd said.

"Well, don't worry. We'll get you home safe. And then everything will be just the way it was before."

Her sudden frown mystified him.

They finished eating and had a little more to drink, and then Stone buried the evil foil packet in the sand. Lily could only hope it didn't sprout an MRE tree. But as horrible as that meatloaf had been, her tummy was full. She was suddenly filled with energy.

"Are you ready to head out?" he asked. His eyes were unusually bright as they fixed on her, but she figured they only seemed so because of the dark camo still streaking his face. She couldn't help wondering what he looked like under all that. His features were sharp and hard, like his name, but she liked the jut of his chin, she liked his high cheekbones and that long straight blade of a nose. His ears were kind of big though. She really liked his neck. It was thick and muscled and the skin there was soft and tanned a toasty brown. His hair was dark and she thought, perhaps, if it weren't so closely cropped, it would curl a little.

His body was long and heavily muscled. At least, she imagined it would be. If he ever took all his gear off. She focused on his chest, trying to imagine—

"Lily?"

"What?"

Oh dear. She should probably stop imagining…

"Are you ready to go?"

She nodded and leaped to her feet.

He picked up his gun and stood as well, though it took a little longer because he was enormous and he was carrying a heavy pack. He teetered backward and she caught him.

Well, she tried to catch him. At the very least she succeeded in slowing his tumble. He landed with an *oof*.

"Shit!" He shot her a remorseful glance. "Sorry, ma'am."

Lily chuckled. "No worries. I've heard that word before on occasion."

"Still. It's not appropriate language around a lady."

"Who told you that?" She tugged on his arm and helped him stand again, though he did most of the work. He pretended to let her help, which she appreciated.

"My mother, of course."

She tipped up her chin and grinned at him, but her grin froze on her lips. She knew he was tall, but…oh my. "Do you…do you always do what your mother tells you to do?"

"Yes, ma'am." His eyes twinkled, so she knew he was telling a lie. But a forgivable one. She responded in kind.

"Me too."

They shared a smile then. It might have lasted a moment or an eternity. Lily shivered as the intensity engulfed her. There was something more to that smile than mere amusement. Almost a touch. Oh, not on a physical level—they were definitely touching, as he had his arm around her shoulder and she had her hand on his chest to steady him—but something else. Something ephemeral.

Then he cleared his throat and looked away and took a tentative step. Then another. Away from her. "Okay," he said. "I'm fine. I'm good to go. Just a little shaky there for a minute."

"Could you have a concussion?"

"No." He shook his head…and winced. "I don't think so. But

we'll take it slow, just to be sure. Ready?"

"Ready, Teddy." She was pretty proud of her use of military vernacular, but he didn't seem impressed. His dark brow came down at a funny angle and he snorted.

Even though he was anxious to leave, he spent a bit of time hunting the area for his helmet, which he didn't find. She could have told him he wouldn't find it. If it had been there, she would have seen it. She was excellent at finding things. Most likely, the pirates had found it on the path last night and taken it, but she didn't mention this possibility to Stone, because he seemed very attached to that helmet.

At long last, he gave up with a gusted sigh. "We should probably head out."

"Okay."

"We'll be moving toward the south," he said, as though that made any difference to her. She was just going to follow. "Keep an eye out for any pirates. And let's keep chatter to a minimum, so I can hear if anyone approaches. Okay?"

Lily crossed her arms over her chest. "I'm not a chatterbox."

"I didn't say you are. It's just that..." He trailed off and then flushed. She knew he flushed because his ears went red.

"It's just that...what?"

"Women like to, I dunno." He shrugged. "Talk."

"Not when we're in mortal danger." Sheesh. Was he one of *those*?

A ripple of chagrin flickered over his features—but only a ripple. "Okay, fine," he clipped.

"Fine." She spun on her heel and marched away.

"Lily?"

Seriously? For someone who was all "we shouldn't talk," he sure didn't wait very long to start a conversation. "What?" She frowned at him over her shoulder.

He pointed down the beach. "The other way."

Her frown darkened. "I knew that," she muttered, and reversed her steps.

All right. He was tall and muscular and smelled really good and his voice was sexy as hell.

But she wasn't sure if she liked him very much after all.

CHAPTER FIVE

Goddamn she was cute when she was in a snit. The way her lips pursed and her nose wrinkled. And the way her hips swung as she sashayed away… There ought to be a law.

It was a damn shame she was the senator's daughter. If she were just a normal girl, she would definitely be the kind of woman he'd make a play for. Oh, not for any kind of long-term thing. But a night?

Fuck yeah.

And then, upon reflection, he changed the night to a weekend in his fantasy. But hell, if it was a fantasy, why stop there? A *week* in bed with her? Doable. Totally doable.

She was doable.

In his fantasies.

But only there.

In real life, no way.

He was a SEAL, dedicated to serving his country. Relationships were tough when a guy was off on missions or running maneuvers. More than a handful of his buddies were divorced because their wives couldn't take the stress of not knowing if their husbands were alive or dead. Not knowing where he was, or if he was coming home. Not knowing anything. Never knowing…

He'd seen the impact of that incessant uncertainty on a family. And the devastation when a man didn't come home. He'd seen it— up close and personal. Mom had never been quite the same.

Military careers were hell on marriages. It took a special kind of strength to take it.

Stone had resolved long ago never to do to a woman what his dad had done to his mom, so relationships were out of the question. Since he also didn't care for one-night stands, that made for a lonely existence.

His lips curled as he thought of the true reason for his nickname. His buddies razzed him when he didn't visit the bars and whorehouses while they were posted overseas, when he didn't avail himself of the services of SEAL groupies at home.

You never get laid, they said. *You must be hard as a stone.*

Well, he was now. Just watching her walk made him hard.

The best he could do was get her to the extraction point, get her off his hands...and then find a nice comfy *happy sock.*

He loved his job. It was always exciting and sometimes as fun as shit. And he liked his life the way it was...with no strings. But damn, if ever there was a woman who might tempt him to want more—

What the fuck? He yanked the reins on his wayward thoughts.

Enough. Enough of this shit.

He was here to perform a mission and that was it.

Not to stare at her ass or enjoy the feel of her in his arms or fucking sniff her hair.

Maybe he did have a concussion. A little one at least. Something had knocked him for a loop.

He caught up to her and yanked her arm, tugging her to the right, into the shadows of the trees. It was a better position to see any oncoming threats without being exposed. He probably shouldn't have yanked so hard. She shot him a wounded look, but he ignored it.

It was his job to protect her and that was what he was going to do.

Even if it meant protecting her from himself.

Especially that.

He was grumpy.

Lily had no idea why he was so grumpy, but she chalked it up to the fact that he probably had one heck of a headache. And maybe a concussion.

Or maybe he was just naturally grumpy.

He was certainly cold. Detached. Unemotional. Like a machine.

She glanced at him from beneath her lashes. With all that goo on his face, it was hard to read his expression, but she could tell he was constantly scanning for threats as they made their way south along the fringe of the trees. Every now and again, he would freeze and hold up his fist. She had no idea what that meant. It was probably SEAL code for...*something*. But after a couple times, she figured out it meant: *Stop walking and twiddle your thumbs until I decide it is time to walk again.*

It was hot, and there were swarms of bugs everywhere—some of them bit—but Lily just pushed through the discomfort. Occasionally, he would stop and they would drink from the little hose on his shoulder. She didn't take much, because she had no idea how much water he had, or how long it needed to last. He hadn't mentioned how big this island was or how far they might need to walk.

She saw neither hide nor hair of the pirates. After a while, she assumed they'd either been killed in the raid or had fled the island...or were waiting up ahead. Thoughts of her fellow captives plagued her. There had been a lot of bullets flying around last night, but she'd been far too frightened to pay close attention. She hoped Brandy and the others were safe, but until they got off this island, she wouldn't know for certain.

Stone slowed as they approached a break in the trees. He motioned for her to stay back as he crept ahead to scout the clearing and make sure it was safe to pass. While as a general rule, Lily did not appreciate being told to stay, like a dog, she was willing to cooperate in this instance.

She sat down on a hummock of dirt and pulled off her shoes while he scuttled to the clearing. She dumped out the sand and massaged her toes, glancing back the way they'd come. How far had they walked? Four miles? Five? Tough to tell but judging from the position of the sun, it was early afternoon.

Her stomach growled as she slipped her shoes back on. She thought dreamily of the meatloaf she'd mocked this morning. What she wouldn't give for a small bite of it now—

She stilled as a twig snapped behind her. Horror rose like lava in her throat. Stone was too far away to have doubled back so quickly. She whirled around, but far too late. Someone grabbed her and covered her mouth with a grimy hand. Someone wiry and strong. Someone who smelled very much like rotten tangerines and sweat.

Her scream was muffled by his palm. She tasted the filth on his fingers. He yanked her against his bony form; his body heat burned her. He snarled something in her ear, something she didn't understand…but she recognized his voice.

Kaafi. The mean one.

With panic whipping through her, she fought as he tried to drag her into the trees. If he succeeded, Stone might not be able to find her. But Kaafi was bigger than her and stronger. She could tell from the nasty odor clinging to him that he'd been chewing qat, the pirate's drug of choice.

As she struggled, something hard hit her side and she realized his rifle was slung over his shoulder. If she could just reach it…

He swung her around and towed her into the woods, but because he had to keep one hand over her mouth, he wasn't very effective. She grabbed for trees and roots and bushes…anything she could to slow them down.

But she'd forgotten how mean he could be.

The hard slam of his fist to her cheek reminded her. It rang through her skull like a claxon. A very excruciating claxon. She crumpled as the pain blinded her. Kaafi grunted with satisfaction, then took her by the wrists and dragged her deeper into the trees. It occurred to her, through the fog, she could scream now, and she tried, but no sound came out.

Her mind spun, her nerves shrieked, she rolled in and out of consciousness, but she was aware of several things. First, she was aware of frustration. She hated being weak and small and unable to protect herself from men like this. Second, she was aware—in spotty bits—of the beauty of the sun angling through the trees. Finally, she was aware that when Kaafi stopped, it was in the middle of the woods. He dropped her on the dirt and hunched down to grin at her. His teeth were brown, his breath bilious. She was still stunned from his punch, but not so stunned that she did not know the cold grip of terror when he ripped open her blouse.

Captain Garnier had assured them that Somali pirates left the women alone. But he'd also said they didn't murder their hostages. These pirates had killed Pierre without hesitation when he'd tried to escape. Shot him down like a dog.

Judging from the glint in Kaafi's eye, he didn't give a rat's ass for pirate conventions.

He dropped his rifle on the ground out of reach and forced her legs apart with his knees. Revulsion licked through her as he shoved his hand between her thighs. His chuckle was dark and foul. She jerked away, rolled from one side to another and hit and clawed and fought until he captured both her wrists in one hand and slapped her again, snarling in clipped and thickly accented English, "Be good."

"No," she wailed.

No. She'd been good her whole life.

She was tired of being good.

So she did something very impolite.

She kneed him in the groin.

His eyes bugged out and he sprayed spittle over her face, but he rolled off her, which was what she wanted.

What she didn't intend was to enrage him.

They didn't tell you about that in self-defense classes…or maybe they had.

He lurched up on his knees and then struggled to his feet, though nearly doubled over and groaning in pain. The muscles on his neck stood out. His nostrils flared. The glare he shot her burned.

He bent down, picked up his rifle, and pointed it at her chest. "No good. You die," he said in a cold voice.

And he pulled the trigger.

The click echoed through the clearing, but Lily barely heard it over the pounding of her pulse. Kaafi turned the gun and frowned at it. He smacked it a couple times, pulled out the round, and reloaded it…and then pointed the rifle at her again.

Lily squeezed her eyes closed and turned her head away. She didn't know a lot about guns, but the bullet had looked pretty big. She wondered what it would feel like, ripping through her body.

She hoped it was quick.

She flinched as the gun fired. The sound was not what she expected. Not a loud bang, but a soft whizz and a dull thud…and then a not so dull thud.

It didn't hurt at all.

Slowly, she cracked open a lid and peeped at Kaafi. He was crumpled on the ground, his eyes open, staring up at the beautiful shafts of light filtering through the leaves. A bubble of blood pooled on his forehead, and then trickled into his hairline.

Lily grabbed her chest to check, to make sure she wasn't shot. Or perhaps to remind her heart it was okay to start beating again.

The brush rustled and she leaped to her feet, angling herself behind the skinny tree. It was probably stupid of her. The tree didn't really provide much cover, but she felt better having it between her and—

Her breath gushed out as Stone appeared.

He barreled toward her at a full run and yanked her into his arms. "Jesus," he gusted. "Are you okay, Lily?"

Okay? He was here. He had saved her. Everything was wonderful. She clung to him like a limpet.

"Yes. Yes." Were those tears dampening her cheeks? Why? Why now? When she was safe? She peered up at him, attempting to blink them away. He froze as their gazes locked. His attention flicked downward, to her breasts cupped in the lace of her bra. His throat worked.

"I thought... I thought... Aw, shit."

And then he kissed her. Hard. Wild. His mouth was hot and sweet and demanding as he took hers. Tantalizing. Delicious. In that harsh coupling, she tasted a savage rejoicing. And she gave it right back.

She'd nearly died. But for a jammed round she would have.

Exhilaration, delight, joy to be alive consumed her.

Or it might have been the kiss.

It was a mighty fine kiss.

It ended far too soon.

Stone pulled back and stared down at her, his chest working like a bellows, as though he'd run a mile. He threaded his fingers through her hair. "Lily," he said, his lips tweaking in the ghost of a smile. "I'm so glad you are not dead."

She grinned at him and repeated his jest from this morning. "I'm glad too."

He missed the joke. Indeed, he frowned. "When I saw his rifle pointed at you, my heart stopped. I was out of range, I had to run...and then, when I saw him shoot—shit." He kissed her again, this one quick and hungry.

"But you got him. You got him." She set her palm on his cheek, ignoring all the shoe polish. No doubt it was all over her face now too. She didn't care. "Thank you for saving me."

"Saving you? I should never have left you alone." He turned away and raked his scalp with his nails. "What the hell was I thinking?"

"You were doing your job. Stone... Stone..." She turned him

back. "I'm fine. We're fine…"

"You almost died."

"But I didn't. Look at me." She held out her arms.

He gaped at her. His eyes glazed over. She realized her chest was totally exposed.

She didn't care, because when his gaze met hers again, there was a new light in it. This light was not detached or cold in the least. It scorched her. Lit something within her.

She'd almost been raped and she'd almost been killed, but somehow all that paled next to the realization that she'd almost died without knowing *this*. His kiss. This *passion*. A raging need snarled through her, a blazing arousal she didn't care to explore. She wanted him. Wanted him more than her next breath. And he wanted her.

"Stone…"

The sizzling moment shattered. He jerked back, as though suddenly reminded of where they were, of the threat that still loomed. He frowned down at Kaafi's body. "We should…go."

Disappointment ravaged her; she attempted to swallow it. She wanted to kiss him again. She wanted him to touch her. She wanted…more. Everything.

But he was probably right. If Kaafi was out here in the woods, there could be others too. And making love next to a dead body, probably not awesome. So when he tugged her lapels together, she let him, and then she tied her blouse under her breasts. Her bra still peeped out when she moved, but a bra was little less than a bikini top, wasn't it?

He forced his gaze away and picked up Kaafi's rifle. "Do you know how to use this?" he asked.

"I've never shot a gun." Lily shrugged. "Point and pull the trigger?"

"It's not a *gun*. It's a rifle or a weapon," he said with a tight smile. Then he showed her how to check for a round, clear the chamber, and switch off the safety, all in quick, practiced moves. It seemed so simple when he did it.

"Keep this," he said, handing it to her. "Just in case."

She snorted. "It's hardly reliable."

Did he need to grin like that? "The point of having a weapon," he said, "is to discourage people from using theirs on you. Keep it. And use it if you need to."

She glanced at the body lying in the dirt. She didn't think she could ever kill someone, but she kept the rifle. He was probably right. If she had it, she would be safer than if she did not. She slung the rifle over her shoulder, as he had his, and followed him back to the beach.

They emerged in the clearing he'd been scouting. It was a good thing he'd thought to do so. The pirates had set up something of a base camp here. Lily could see the remains of a fire, a pile of suitcases, and a cache of food and water from the *Avonturier*.

Stone kept watch as she found a backpack and filled it with canned food, water bottles, antiseptic hand wipes, and a first aid kit. From her own suitcase, she grabbed another pair of shoes, clean underwear, and a fresh shirt, though she didn't bother to change here—they had to hurry in case the pirates came back. She would have taken more, but the pack was getting heavy.

"Ready?" Stone asked, his voice slithering toward her on a whisper. She nodded and tossed him a bottle of water. He opened it and drank it down in one go. She did the same. It felt wonderful, so she grabbed another.

"Not too much," he cautioned. "Too much might upset your stomach."

Seriously? All this and he was worried about an upset stomach?

His brows came down. "If you throw up, you could become dehydrated."

"Oh." Of course.

He jerked his head toward the beach. She was beginning to understand his language. That jerk meant: *Let's go*.

She bit back a grin and followed him.

They moved a little slower, because of her. The added weight of the backpack made her feet sink into the sand, but he didn't seem to mind. He kept pace with her, scanning the beach and the tree line with constant vigil.

It must be exhausting, being him.

But then, it was exhausting being her. At least, at the moment.

She was glad she hadn't had that second bottle of water when her belly churned. "Can...can we stop for a minute?" she panted.

His mottled brow wrinkled and then he nodded crisply. "Not for long." He checked the sky. Evening was coming. They'd walked all day.

Her thighs screamed. She told them to shut up.

Stone found a fallen log and gestured for her to sit. He, however, stood, facing the woods and glaring into the foliage. Did he never relax? She sighed and fished around for the antiseptic wipes, taking the opportunity to scrub her face and hands. To her mortification, the wipe came back black. She frowned at him. "Why didn't you tell me I was covered in shoe polish?"

He rocked back on his heels. "'Cause it was cute?"

She tried to glower, but it was difficult. He thought she was cute.

"And it's not shoe polish."

"It looks like shoe polish. Here." She thrust a wipe at him. "You should clean up too."

"I'm on a mission. We get dirty."

She blew out a breath. "I mean, your face."

"It's better if I leave it on."

Seriously? "It's scary looking."

"It's *supposed* to be scary looking."

"It gets all over me when you kiss me."

He froze. His gaze locked on her lips. His tongue peeped out…as though he was thinking about that kiss. Or thinking about kissing her again.

A thrill shot through her.

"I, ah, shouldn't have done that. I'm sorry, ma'am."

Annoyance riffled. "Oooh. Don't call me ma'am. Old ladies are ma'am."

"It's a sign of respect."

"No, it's not. You say it when you want to create distance between us."

"There should be distance between us. I'm on a mission." She didn't like the way his voice raised, the way it lit with emotion. Or maybe she did.

"You said that before."

"It's still true. I'm a goddamn SEAL. You're my mission. Getting you home safe. That's all that matters."

"You're also a man."

He clamped his jaw shut and stared at her. Silence throbbed between them. Then he said, in a hard, cold voice, "I am not a man. I'm a weapon. And I am definitely not the man for you."

It could have been her imagination, but she didn't think it was, that tiny thread of regret in his tone.

Still, his words hurt. "You kissed me." An accusation.

"It was purely an emotional reaction. I thought he'd killed you. I thought he'd fucking raped you and killed you…"

"So…you kissed me?"

"It was the adrenaline. Nothing more."

She hid her smile, digging in the dirt with her toe. "Do you kiss all the people you save?"

"What? Hell no—" He stopped short, realizing what he'd just admitted, realizing how much he'd revealed with that enflamed denial.

She lifted her gaze to his. "So why did you kiss me?" she asked softly, but he heard. He scrubbed his face with a palm. A pity only some of the shoe polish came off.

He hunkered down and gusted a sigh. "That should be obvious, shouldn't it?"

"Should it?" It wasn't. Not really. She *hoped* she knew what it meant, but he was so hard to read, she couldn't be sure unless he said it.

"You're a…" He waved a hand at her.

"Woman."

"A woman. Yes. And I'm a…"

"Man." This much, she already knew. "So, you kiss all the *women* you rescue."

"Of course not."

"Do you kiss *any* of the women you rescue?"

He frowned. "I kissed you."

"Anyone else?"

His frown turned into a glower. He stood in a rush. "We should get going."

She stretched out her legs and crossed them at the ankles. "Anyone else?"

"Lily. Come on. We've rested long enough."

Right. She wasn't going anywhere until she got her answer. She tipped her head and arched a brow.

There was no need for him to growl.

She did not allow herself to be intimidated. She growled right back.

This seemed to stun him, for some reason. As though he was used to people just snapping to attention and doing his bidding. Silly rabbit.

"By the way," she murmured in a casual tone. "I can be very stubborn." She tweaked a grin at him. "They say it runs in the family."

"I could pick you up and carry you."

Such an empty threat. "Me and this heavy pack and your pack and… My, my, Stone. How far do you think we'd get?"

"Goddamn it, Lily—"

"Any. One. Else?"

"You are stubborn, aren't you?"

"Anyone else?"

"No! Okay. No. Never. Not even one goddamn time."

She studied him, relishing in his confession. Then she stood and collected her things. She patted him on the shoulder. "See? That wasn't so hard, was it?"

He muttered something that sounded like, *"You have no fucking idea."*

Whirling to hide her smirk, she sauntered away.

"Lily?"

She glanced at him over her shoulder. "Hmm?"

He jammed his thumb down the beach. "The other way."

Oh. *Right.*

Shooting him a supercilious look, she wheeled around and resumed the trek to the south.

CHAPTER SIX

He shouldn't have kissed her. He shouldn't have.

But damn, he was glad he had.

If nothing else, he knew how she tasted.

And she tasted incredible.

But that was it. That was all it could ever be.

Hell, he'd nearly lost all control. Nearly forgotten where they were and laid her down on the ground and fucked her—right there in the scrub.

She deserved better. A bed at least.

Dinner. Candlelight. Romance.

What was he thinking?

She deserved better than *him*.

Lily Wilson was the kind of woman who belonged at a fancy tea party surrounded by high society or celebrities. Her father was one of the most elite politicians in the country. He probably had a goddamn prince picked out for his daughter. Not a guy like Stone who drove a 4x4 and had a crappy little house in a suburb of Seattle that he visited far too infrequently. He only kept it because it was close to Mom.

Lily Wilson deserved a well-educated, sophisticated husband. A rich husband who could fly her to the South of France for her birthday. Or could buy her a BMW. Diamonds...

He'd never shopped for diamonds. He wondered how much they cost. Probably a lot—

But it didn't fucking matter.

He wasn't buying diamonds for her...or anyone.

48

He wasn't that kind of guy.

And she deserved better.

Oh sure, she'd been all soft and willing. In fact, she'd met his passion and surpassed it...but he knew. He knew how reaction could hit a person. That was all it had been. Reaction. Relief. That scorching thrill when a deadly threat is vanquished.

A man wanted to revel in those times, when the blood ran high. To ravage and pillage and take what he wanted.

Making love in a moment like that would be a natural response as adrenaline pumped through the veins.

She might *think* she wanted him, wanted *it*, but she was wrong. When she was out of this situation, back to her normal life, she wouldn't even glance at a guy like him.

He was an idiot for even thinking about it.

They rounded a corner and the tumult of his thoughts stalled. The unmistakable outline of huts showed through the trees. He held up a fist and hunkered down. She mimicked his actions.

That was the thing about Lily. She was a quick study. And she was smart. And pretty. And she smelled—

He cut off the thought with a frown.

It didn't matter how she smelled—*like sex on a stick*—it only mattered that she was smart. And followed orders. And—

A call wafted from the village. He narrowed his eyes and stared through the dusky shadows at the clearing. Three pirates moved around the huts, collecting weapons. A tall, skinny one was dragging something to a pile on the far side of the village. Stone's pulse jerked when he realized what it was.

A body.

In uniform.

There were other bodies in the pile too. From what he could see, most were wearing the scraggy clothes of the pirates. While anger roiled that the other teams had also lost at least one man on this mission, he was relieved there weren't more. It pissed him off to see a pirate pick up the fallen SEAL's weapon and check it over.

The idiot jerked back as he pulled the trigger, sending an accidental spray of bullets through the compound. Without thought, Stone put his arm around Lily's shoulders and pulled her lower. He didn't want her hit by a stray round because these morons didn't know how to handle a weapon.

That the pirate laughed, rankled.

The urge rose in him to do them all, just lift his weapon and let the bullets fly, but he knew better. For one thing, SEALs had a code—they only used lethal force when a team member or a hostage was in mortal danger. And for another, wasting a band of scavenger pirates wasn't his mission.

He tugged Lily back and into the trees. "We need to wait here until dark," he whispered. "And then sneak past."

She nodded, her eyes wide. Trusting.

He hoped he would prove worthy of that trust.

As they waited, he watched the tide, as he'd been doing all day. They were close to the southernmost tip of the island. Close to safety. Low tide was the best time to cross. He checked his watch and calculated when it would be safest. That it would be in the middle of the night was a blessing. With any luck, it would be pitch-black again tonight, but it didn't much matter. They had to get to the extraction point come hell…or high water.

To do that, they needed to slither past this village and over to the southern promontory and then slip into the water without being seen.

And Lily couldn't swim.

He glanced at her. Her eyes were closed, her face wan.

She seemed so fragile, he wanted to gather her up into his arms and hold her.

Damn. He shouldn't have glanced at her.

He forced his gaze back to the sea, but it kept drifting to her.

In the end, he just gave up and watched her. Stared at her. Studied her.

It pained him, the soul-deep denial that *this* was all he got. But still, he watched her until the sun set and it was too dark to make out the lines of her face.

Which was fine.

By then, he'd memorized them.

It was full-on dark by the time Stone motioned they should move out; the moon was but a wraith, hiding behind the clouds. He still didn't speak, despite the fact the pirates had all left the village.

They skulked through the shadows and around the tip of the

island. He pointed toward the water and made a motion with his hand. She didn't know how she knew he was telling her they would wait for the tide to go out, but she did. The other island was little more than a hulking hump on the horizon. It seemed terribly far. Too far to swim, for certain.

Stone sloughed off his gear and unbuckled his vest. Before she realized what he intended, he strapped it around her.

"What are you doing?" she hissed.

"Shh."

She frowned at him. "*You* need this."

"If the water gets too deep, I'll have to take you piggyback and carry you. When that happens, your back will be to the shore. Keep your head down."

Horror curled through her.

Not only did she have to ford a seemingly endless stretch of cold, deep water...there was the possibility of being shot at while doing it.

"Oh no. No." He needed to wear the body armor. For one thing, it was heavy enough to make her sink to the bottom like a rock. For another...what would she do if anything happened to him? She couldn't bear it. Especially not if he died keeping her safe. She fiddled with the fastenings to remove it, but her fingers were numb. He set his big hand over hers and stilled her movements.

His eyes met hers; they glowed in the night. "You must wear this. I insist."

"But—"

"Ah ah ah." He silenced her with a finger to her lips. "I'm stubborn too, Lily."

She believed him. So she left the armor on...and prayed the decision didn't kill both of them.

When he judged the timing to be right, when he determined the pirates were not around, he nodded and they set out. They moved quickly, but only as quickly as she could go wearing the heavily plated vest. Unbelievably, he took her pack and carried it, along with his own, on his back. His weapon, he held in his hand at the ready. They crouched and dashed across the spit of land arching toward the sea.

There were no trees for cover here, but the sand was firm and it was easy to move.

Lily was just starting to feel cocky when they reached the shore.

She should never feel cocky.

A sudden fear scudded through her as she stared at the distance to the other island. She'd never make it. She never would.

He looked down at her as she hesitated. "It's okay," he said. "I'm here."

And as easily as that, her trepidation fled. He was here. Stone was here. He would take care of her. She knew it.

So she waded with him into the water, refusing to freak out as the licking waves consumed her ankles, then her knees, and then her waist.

He shot her a reassuring grin. "How're you doing?"

"Fine." Not. But she didn't want to disappoint him by quailing. The water hit her breasts. They were in the tropics, but still, it was chilly. She shivered as it reached her neck. They weren't yet halfway there. "Stone?"

He stopped and surveyed the situation. The water didn't even reach his chest. How fair was that? Without a word, he bent down and she clambered onto his back, clinging to his pack. She wished he weren't wearing it. She wished they could be melded together, body to body.

"Remember," he murmured, "head down." And then he forged onward.

A cry went up from the shore. Lily glanced back and saw a lone figure waving his arms. Then it bent. Picked something up.

"Stone?"

A shot rang out. It went wide.

Unbelievably, Stone chuckled. He spun around, lifted his weapon, and fired. The shadow fell.

Lily struggled for breath. Oh God. *Oh God.* She smacked his shoulder. "What the hell do you think you're doing?"

He snorted. "Taking care of business."

"You shouldn't have turned. You're not protected."

He waggled his rifle. "*This* is my protection."

"Don't do that again."

"I will if I need to."

"Don't. I don't want you to get hurt."

"Oh, and it's okay if you take a bullet?"

"I'm wearing body armor."

"I don't give a shit. If I feel the need to shoot at a fucking pirate, I'm going to shoot at a fucking pirate."

Why he sounded so grumpy, she had no clue, but she let the topic drop because the shoreline sloped and, with no warning, they were both neck deep in water. "Take this," he said as he handed her her backpack. She nearly dropped it, but then tightened her hold and looped it over her shoulder. "I'm going to start swimming. Hang on."

Hang on?

Okay.

She clung to the straps of his backpack and closed her eyes for good measure. Thank God he was big. Thank God he was strong. She couldn't imagine swimming like this, with a full pack and another person weighing her down. The thought made her breathless. Or perhaps that was the temperature of the water. For now they were in the ocean—*in the ocean*—and it was very cold.

His movements were smooth and he swam slowly, as though there was no urgency. She suspected it was for her benefit. She vowed to make him proud. Or as proud as she could.

She held on and tried to float so she wouldn't be too much of a burden; she found she rather enjoyed the sensation of gliding through the water. Maybe, when she got home, her next adventure would be swimming lessons. That was probably the extent of her courage, after this.

The hulking shadow grew, which Lily found reassuring. The waves slapped them, the current tugged and pulled, but he kept on target, swimming like a guided missile toward the shore. She felt his shivers. The tremble of his weakening muscles, but he didn't so much as pause. She hoped to God they reached the island before he ran out of steam.

When his motion shifted and he straightened to stand, she let out a breath she didn't realize she'd been holding. Her head went light.

"Almost there." His voice was low and soothing, but she heard the strain in it.

"You're wonderful," she whispered into his ear. She liked to think his burst of speed was a result of her praise, but she was probably delusional. He continued to carry her until the water reached his chest, and then he guided her as she slid off his back. She hated letting go but he'd carried her far enough. "Well," she huffed. "That was exciting."

"You did well." He tucked a hank of wet hair behind her ear. "Come on. Let's get ashore. Remember to keep your head down."

She laughed. "There are no pirates here."

"We don't know that." He frowned. "Let's operate as though there are. Be on the safe side. Okay?" He chucked her chin.

She tried not to glower. She wasn't a baby. "Fine."

"We'll head inland. Find a place to hole up for the night, and tomorrow the cavalry will come."

"Promise?"

"Promise." He smiled when he said it, so it must be true.

As they emerged onto the shore, Stone's every muscle ached. He ignored his fatigue. He knew, if he pushed through it, it would wane and he'd get his second wind. Besides, he wouldn't relax until he knew they were safe. He hadn't been kidding when he'd mentioned there could be pirates on this island. As far as he knew, they were everywhere.

He glanced at Lily; her shivers concerned him. The night was balmy, but they were wet through and through, and the breeze had a chilling effect. He knew her shaking wasn't only because of the cold. She'd been a real trooper through all this, but now reaction was setting in. The last thing he needed was for her to crumble. He decided to distract her.

"Well, that wasn't so bad," he gusted. "Hardly a nibble."

Lily paled even more. *Shit.* Maybe he should have picked a different way to distract her. Kiss her or—

"What-what do you mean, hardly a nibble?"

He looked out over the water just as a fin rose in the surf. "Um. Nothing?"

"What did you mean?" Her gaze followed his. She *eeped.* "Were there *sharks* out there?"

"Only a few. And they weren't hungry."

Why she smacked him—again—he had no clue. Or he did. But it was a relief to see her lips quirk. "Dang it, Stone. You should have told me."

"Told you?" He shifted his pack and checked his weapon. Then he took hers, tipped it up and poured the water from the muzzle. The firing mechanisms on the AKs were supposed to be watertight. He hoped they wouldn't have to test it soon. "Would you have wanted to know?"

She wrinkled her nose. Then grinned. "No. But still…"

He chuckled at her expression, suffused by a sudden lightness. Funny, that was all it took—a grin from her and all was well with the world. "Come on. Let's find shelter."

He led Lily inland, encouraging her to stay low until they hit the cover of the trees. The darkness that had shielded them on their swim was now annoying. What he wouldn't give for his night-vision goggles, but he'd lost them when he'd lost his helmet.

Still, he moved as quietly as he could through the scrub, forging deeper until he found a U-shaped rock formation, which he determined would provide good cover.

"We'll stay the night here," he said as he dropped his pack. She dropped hers as well and started riffling through it, pulling out water and food without him needing to ask. He liked that about her.

He went through his pack too, stuffing a couple energy bars into his pocket. When he pulled out his thermal blanket and a packet of condoms fell on the ground, Stone grimaced. Goddamn Garrett. Condoms were not standard issue for a mission, but it was a standing joke in the platoon. The guys loved to razz him about being a Fucking Monk—literally. A *fucking monk*. More than once he'd found the damn things hidden in his pack.

He wasn't prepared for the effect of seeing them fall out, here and now.

Thoughts, visions, fantasies whipped through him, all of them with a disturbing result. Though he was wet and clammy and cold, a sear of heat licked him. He shoved the packets back into the pocket and ripped open the plastic bag holding the thermal blanket. He billowed it out and wrapped it around her shoulders.

"What about you?" she asked.

"I'm fine."

"You're wet. You must be cold."

He was. But there was still a lot of work to do before he could relax. He tossed her the P-38. She studied it. "What's this?"

He picked up his weapon. "A can opener. Pick out a couple things to eat. I'll be back in a bit."

Her eyes went wide. "Where are you going?"

"I'm going to scout around. Make sure we're alone. With these rock formations, you're well hidden and this is a defensible position. You'll be safe. You go ahead and eat. Don't forget to drink. If everything looks good, maybe I'll make a fire when I get back. Do you have any dry clothes?"

She shook her head. "They're all wet."

"Okay. Lay them out. Hopefully they'll dry by morning. Keep that blanket on. Stay quiet. And..." He picked up the rifle they'd confiscated from the pirate in the woods and handed it to her. "Use this if you need to. I'll whistle when I approach." A wink. "Please don't shoot me."

She gave a heavy sigh, but her lips tweaked in a mischievous smile. "I'll try not to."

"Right. I'll be back soon."

"Right."

He should go—he needed to secure the area—but he was loath to leave her. She was so small and wan, so delicate.

She parted her lips just then. Her tongue peeped out. He couldn't rip his gaze away; it tangled with hers. The moment hung between them.

"Stone..." She took a step toward him. And he toward her.

He shouldn't do this. He really shouldn't, but he couldn't stop himself. He pulled her into his arms and he kissed her, consumed her. A hard, desperate melding of mouths. He never wanted it to end.

But he yanked away. Shook his head.

Fuck.

"I'm..."

She cut his apology off with a palm to his cheek. "Stone." A whisper. "Come back safe."

"I will." Before he grabbed her again and kissed her again and got distracted again, he whirled away. "I'll be back."

He had to force himself to focus as he made his way to the beach and around the perimeter of the island. It was much smaller than the one they'd left, a mere spit, and he was relieved to see no signs of habitation...or hostiles. His thoughts kept drifting back to Lily, that kiss, and the condoms in his pack.

Damn Garrett.

Knowing they were there was a fucking irritant.

His main brain knew nothing could ever happen between him and the senator's daughter. His secondary brain...well, it wasn't on the same page. The constant flare of arousal when he thought of her annoyed him. He'd never been distracted by a woman. Not ever. But something about Lily Wilson burrowed under his skin, touched him at his core.

He'd always been disdainful of guys who were blinded by lust or weakened by love. Probably because he hadn't understood how hard it could hit a guy.

Whoa. Wait.

He wasn't in love, for fuck's sake. This was lust. Pure and simple. Nothing more.

But there was nothing simple about it.

The emotions she engendered in him were a tangled mess.

Indeed, this pass through the island served as more than a scouting mission. It was a chance for Stone to gain control of his wayward thoughts. To get ahold of these burgeoning yearnings. To get himself back to center.

By the time he returned to her, he was feeling confident and strong. They were alone here, at least for the time being. And he was going to resist kissing her again.

If it killed him.

When the little voice at the back of his mind whispered, "It probably will," he told it to shut up.

CHAPTER SEVEN

Lily hated this.

Oh, she'd hated a lot of things since their boat had been seized. Seeing Pierre die, certainly. The rough treatment by some of the pirates. The hunger. The odors. Sleeping on the hard ground. The fear.

But this was the worst of it. Sitting on a rock, huddled in a silver blanket, waiting. Not knowing. Was he safe? When would he be back? What would she do if he didn't return? How many bullets were in her rifle?

When her thoughts became too alarming, she distracted herself by collecting sticks and dried brush, in case Stone wanted to make a fire, and then she opened some cans and had a bit to eat. It took her a while to figure out his can-opener thingy. She had no idea why it had to be so difficult, but once she got the hang of it, she felt as though she had conquered the world.

She saved the lion's share of each can for Stone, because he would be hungry when he returned.

Because it was dark, and the cans were marked in a language she didn't understand, it was a strange mélange. Certainly not a dinner she would ever prepare at home. Surprisingly, the canned tuna went well with the mangos. Still…not a meal she would choose again.

The nuts were far more satisfying. Probably because she was craving salt. Remembering Stone's admonition, she drank a bottle of water. With the first sip, she realized she was horrifically thirsty, but she made herself drink slowly.

Then, when her tummy was full, and the thermal blanket did its work, wrapping her in warmth, exhaustion set in.

She didn't want to sleep—in case someone other than Stone crept up on their position—but it probably wouldn't hurt to rest her eyes. A bit.

The sounds of the night surrounded her. The slap of waves on the shore was little more than a distant whisper, but the island was alive with rustles and chirps. They were soothing. Or, perhaps she was pooped. It had been a very long day. She yawned, settled back against the rock and closed her eyes.

She snapped awake as a shrill whistle cut through the air. Her heart leaped. Leaped and danced with joy. Elation washed through her. He was back. He was back!

He emerged from the shadows looking like a warrior of old. Oh, she couldn't see any details, but his outline was striking and familiar and somehow very dear.

Though they'd met little more than a day ago, Lily couldn't help feeling she'd known him forever.

He hunkered down at her side and studied her. "How are you doing?"

"I'm…good." Their gazes locked. Thoughts of that kiss, those kisses, wafted through her brain. She wanted to kiss him again. She wanted…more than that. "Are we safe?"

He nodded, dropping his rifle on his backpack and settling beside her. "For now. Are you cold?"

"A little. Are you?" A quick scan showed his clothes were drier than hers, but they were still damp.

He grunted and arranged the firewood she'd collected in the vee of the rocks, where it wouldn't be spotted. "There's a marine layer coming in, so it should be safe to have a fire." He glanced at her. "No one will see the smoke."

She shivered. "A fire would be nice."

He went through his bag, pulled out a flint and quickly got a blaze going. When she shuttled closer, he held her back. "Don't get too close. Don't want you getting singed."

She shot him a playful smile. "I'm a grown-up, Stone. I know how to play with fire." She let the blanket fall and held out her hands, soaking in the warmth.

"Do you?" He seemed amused. He picked up the wipes and

cleaned his hands with one. It came away almost black. He used another to scour his face and the back of his neck, gusting a sigh. "Damn, that feels good."

Lily didn't respond. She couldn't. She was addlepated.

Oh, she'd known he was handsome. She could tell from the lines of his face. But in the light of the flickering fire, with all the goo wiped away, he was breathtaking. A powerful, jutting chin, high cheekbones, feathery lashes, and sharp gray eyes. His forehead was broad, his nose straight and long, and his lips... Oh, holy heaven. His lips. Full and lush and delectable.

All her tiredness fled. She was swamped with the hum of a new energy.

He was handsome and tall. Strong. A hero. His voice rumbled in a seductive, gravelly purr. He was perfect.

She'd never felt desire like this. Not for any other man. Ever.

While she reveled in the fire and pretended not to stare at him, he ate. And ate. And ate.

Dang, the man could eat.

When he set down the last can, he issued a roiling belch, then sent her a repentant look. On him, it was unbearably cute. "Sorry," he said.

She grinned at him. "Was it that good?"

He snorted a laugh. "It was filling. And better than an MRE, I guess."

She shuddered. "That meatloaf was hideous."

"You should try the chicken fajita meal. Now *that* is hideous."

Silence hummed between them as he tidied up the cans. She wanted, needed, to break it. "How long have you been a SEAL?" she asked.

"Seven years." It annoyed her that he avoided her gaze.

"That's a long time."

"It is."

"I bet you've seen some things."

He stilled, his eyes shadowed with memories. "I have."

Seriously? She was trying to make conversation. Could he answer with more than two-word responses? "Why did you join?"

He blew out a breath. "You ask a lot of questions."

"I'm interested. Why did you join?"

"Because my father was a SEAL, I guess. I was raised as a navy brat. It seemed logical. And… It's always been my passion."

"Hmm. Do you have siblings? What do they do?"

Oh dear. She shouldn't have asked. A dark curtain came down over his features. His jaw bunched. She thought he would refuse to answer, but he said, "I have a sister. She's a civvie. A writer, of all things." He gave a grunt, as though being a writer was an incongruous choice. "And I have a brother."

"A brother? Is he a SEAL too?"

"He is. One of the best."

"Where is he now?"

"San Diego. He's training recruits." Stone chuckled, but then his expression darkened. "And then there's Drake."

Lily tipped her head to the side. "Who's Drake? Another brother?"

He frowned at her, making her wonder if he regretted mentioning Drake at all. "Not by blood, but we grew up together. Our dads were in the same unit. Our moms were…widowed together."

"I'm sorry."

His muscles flexed as he lifted a shoulder. "It was a long time ago. Anyway, Drake's like a brother to me. He always was an annoying little shit."

"What does he do?"

"SEAL." A harsh laugh. "Aren't we all? He's damn good, though, for an annoying little shit. He's been on some very high-profile missions. Awards up the wazoo."

"And where is he now?"

Stone turned away and began going through his pack. "We should get some rest." He pulled out a plastic bag and ripped it open, slipping out a thin tarp. He laid it down next to the fire. "This will keep the cold of the ground from seeping in."

"Stone?"

"Hmm?"

"Where's Drake?"

He stilled. His throat worked. "He's… I… Shit, Lily. I don't want to talk about this."

"Is he somewhere dangerous? Like Afghanistan?"

"No. Lily…"

"Where?" Had he forgotten how dogged she could be?

"I don't know, okay? He was on this mission, and I hope to God he got out okay, but I don't know." He scrubbed his palm over his scalp. "Shit."

Her heart ached. "I'm sure he's fine."

"Right." He stared at the fire. When he spoke again, his voice was soft, almost a whisper. "Thing is, he was hit. During the raid. I keep wondering, could he make it to the LZ with a bullet in his leg?"

"Is he very much like you?"

Her question stunned him. Stunned him so much he actually looked at her. His eyes were wide, his brow rumpled. "Like me? I suppose. I suppose. Yeah. He's very much like me." He laughed, as if surprised by the realization.

"Then he'll be fine, Stone."

Their gazes locked. A flicker of hope blazed in his expression. "God, he better be. If he's hurt...his mom will kill me. I promised to keep him safe. And I..." He trailed off. His Adam's apple worked.

"He's fine. I'm certain of it."

"It's a dangerous business we're in. A dangerous world."

Lily didn't respond. She couldn't. Her world wasn't dangerous in the slightest. Probably because she was cosseted like a prize poodle. Nothing remotely exciting had ever happened...until now. After a bit, she asked, "Have you ever thought of doing something else?"

He gaped at her as though she'd asked him if he would care to rob a bank. "Something else?"

"With your training, I bet you could."

He shook his head. "I can't imagine what it would be."

"But what do guys like you do, when they leave the service?" You couldn't be a soldier forever.

His laugh was harsh. "I dunno. Curl up and die?"

"There's got to be more to life than this."

"Jumping out of airplanes in the dark and traveling the world? Working with the finest men on the planet?"

"You love it." It was there. In his voice.

"I do. I suppose at some point I'll be too old to keep up." He chuckled. "Maybe I'll become a movie consultant or some shit like that." He winced. "Sorry, ma'am."

"Please don't call me ma'am."

"Sorry." Silence simmered until he slapped his knees and gusted, "So, what do you say? Should we get some rest?"

Her mood dipped. She didn't want rest. She enjoyed talking to

him. Enjoyed watching his lips move as he spoke. She wanted…
Well, she just wanted.

As though she had agreed, he barreled on. "You take the tarp and
the blanket and sleep by the fire."

"What about you?"

"I'll keep watch."

"You need to sleep too."

"No, I don't."

She frowned at him. "Stone…"

"We're trained for sleep deprivation, Lily. It'll be fine. Really. Just
lie down and go to sleep."

Dang it. She'd been fantasizing about curling up…with him. With
all his gear off, she could see the ripple of muscles beneath his t-shirt,
the bulge of his biceps. She'd been hoping to steal another kiss…

But she did as he asked. And tried not to pout. He settled against
the rock near the edge of their little shelter with his rifle on his lap.
He was like a machine. No doubt he would sit there all night.

She watched him until the fire burned down. Watched him and
thought about him. This man who had saved her and kept her safe.
She wanted to repay him. She wanted to give him something back.

Oh, hell. Who was she fooling? She wanted to take.

She wanted *him*. Once they were rescued, there would never be
another chance and she knew it.

It was now or never.

And, while it was true that what would be, would be…it didn't
hurt to tip the odds in her favor. Did it?

Thank God she'd finally settled down.

All through dinner and the conversation that followed, Stone had
been possessed of one thought. Yanking her into his arms and kissing
her. She looked so beautiful in the firelight, her elegant movements,
her expressive features. Her hair.

He wanted to wrap his fist around that hair. He wanted it flowing
over his body. It was all he could do to try to remain detached.

He didn't feel very detached at the moment, but it didn't matter.
She was asleep. He only had to make it through the night. In the
morning the chopper would come and she'd be returned to her father
and he…well, he'd return to his team. What was left of it.

He tried not to think about Zack. About the letter he had to write.

He tried not to think about Drake, because worry for him ate at his gut.

It was much more pleasant to think about Lily. To play out scenarios in his mind where they weren't on a mission and he didn't have obligations and she wasn't a senator's daughter. As pleasant as those thoughts were, they made him uncomfortable. His cock stirred.

Thank God she was asleep—

"Stone?"

He sighed heavily. "Yes, Lily?"

She pushed up onto her elbow and stared at him. The fire was nothing but embers, accentuating her form. "I'm cold."

Well, fuck.

"Will you come over here and lie next to me?"

Double fuck.

"That's not a good idea, Lily." For oh-so-many reasons.

"Why not?"

Because if I lie next to you, I won't be able to keep my fucking hands to myself. "I need to keep watch."

"I thought you said we are safe."

"We are."

Silence settled. Thank—

"But I'm cold."

"Cold?" She had the *blanket.*

"Yes." A tiny voice. Tiny, but compelling. She'd probably been spoiled rotten as a child with that voice. "Won't you come and warm me up?"

Shit. If he didn't know better, he would think she was trying to seduce him.

It would probably have worked.

Goddamn it. He knew it would be a miserable night, but he hadn't anticipated it would go this sour. "All right. Scoot over." He used his gruffest tone, so she would know. She would understand. He was doing this for one reason only. To warm her up.

She edged to the side of the tarp and lifted the blanket. He couldn't help noticing the knot beneath her breasts had come undone as she'd moved around searching for a comfortable position. Her bra peeped out. The sight skewered him.

With a grumble he settled in next to her, making it a point to show her his back. He arranged the blanket so it was mostly covering her and rested his head on his arm.

Damn. She'd lied.

She wasn't cold. She was hot.

Her warmth soaked through him, sending shivers up his spine.

"Thank you, Stone," she whispered. "This is much better."

Better?

Hell.

It was hell.

When she breathed or moved or *thought* about breathing or moving, the scent of her teased his nostrils. He held himself as still as he could, clenching his muscles so he didn't accidentally roll over and fuck her or something.

But damn…

To his horror, she shifted, cuddling closer with a low murmur. She wrapped her arm around his waist and sealed herself to his back. Her soft breasts gouged at his sanity.

"This is nice," she said.

"Mmm." *Nice, my ass.*

"I remember, when we were swimming across the water… Well, you were swimming. I was holding on. But I remember thinking, I wish you weren't wearing that backpack."

What? "Why?"

Yeah. He probably shouldn't have asked. It only encouraged her. She pressed closer. His pulse surged.

"Because I wanted to feel this."

He cleared his throat. "Th-this?"

Her hand raked his chest.

Holy God. Did she have any idea what kind of dragon such a simple touch could unleash? Indeed, he was at full erection in a heartbeat. He caught her hand in his. To stop her. God knew where such an innocent caress could lead.

"Stone…"

With a groan he rolled over and glared at her. Or tried to.

It hardly mattered. She seemed indomitable. Besides, it was far too dark for her to be appropriately cowed. "What?"

He did not expect her response.

Soft fingers fluttering over his cheek, holding him still as her lips found his.

Every muscle in his body seized as she explored his mouth, kissing him, suckling his lower lip, dabbing her tongue in.

He was strong. He was indomitable too. He could hold out. He could—

She roved over his chin to his neck, nuzzling and sucking a tender spot, a spot that made sheets of hot lust rain down on him.

He groaned. "Lily…"

"I want this," she said, sucking on him again, nipping.

"You don't know what you're doing."

She chuckled. "I'm pretty sure I do…"

He grabbed her head, held her still to make his point. It was a very important point. What was it?

Right.

"What you're feeling is a normal reaction."

"I know." She bussed his chin and—God help him—*licked*.

"You've been under a lot of pressure. And now we're nearly home. You're a woman. I'm a man."

"Yes, you are."

Her tone made something, way down deep, harden.

"This is a normal reaction to the situation. Trust me. You'll regret it in the morning."

"I'll regret it more if I miss this." She leaned her forehead on his chest, which was a relief because she stopped kissing him. But then she scraped him. With her nails. When she hit his nipple he almost came out of his skin. "You have no idea what my life is like, Stone."

"Perfect—"

"Far from it. I'm so protected, sometimes I feel like I'm in a cage. Every element of my day is orchestrated."

"I thought you said you were stubborn."

"I am. I think I mentioned it runs in the family?" She peeped up at him and grinned. "My parents can be overwhelming, but I'm not their little girl anymore. I'm determined to live my own life…without their interference. Determined to take what I want." Her naughty smile sent a shiver through him. "I've never had an adventure before now. I've certainly never met a man like you."

"Good. Men like me are—"

She somehow found his Adam's apple as it bobbed, and sucked on that. "Wild. Savage. Sexy…"

Ah. That was it.

Stone's stomach sank. Yeah. She was a groupie. This wasn't about him as a man…it was about him as a SEAL. Why he felt so disappointed, he didn't know. Most guys would just say, *"Thank you very much, ma'am,"* and get on with it.

But somehow, even though it was her, even though it was Lily, and he wanted her with a blazing passion, he couldn't do it.

He started to push away but then she said something that made his resolve crumble.

"You have a great sense of humor. Even when people are shooting at you. And you love your mom. Your family. And you're smart, charming when you want to be—"

"Wait. What? When I want to be?"

"You can be…grumbly."

"I excel at grumbly."

"I noticed."

"It's a gift."

"At any rate…I find you very attractive."

"What if I wasn't draped in full SEAL kit? What if I was wearing overalls or a business suit?"

"I would find you attractive if you were buck naked."

A scorching talon of lust slashed him. "Would you?"

"Oh." She stroked his pec. "Most definitely."

"Lily." He should probably make one more attempt. But he was weakening and, damn, he wanted to weaken.

"Yes, Stone?"

"We shouldn't do this."

"Hmm. You're probably right."

His mood plummeted. On some level, he was already in her.

"But you know what?" she said. "I don't care."

She kissed him again and his mood…rose.

This time, he didn't stop her.

CHAPTER EIGHT

Oh. Heaven. He levered over her and took her mouth in a brutal kiss. Lily reveled in it, giving back as good as she got. He tasted incredible and smelled...so manly. Like wood smoke and sweat and, well, like *Stone*. Her heart thudded, her mind reeled. Lust blossomed.

She wanted him. Now.

Like a wild woman, she scored his chest, his scalp, sank her nails into his bulging biceps. He groaned and pulled her closer. His large hand skimmed up her abdomen until he cupped her breast and squeezed. Delight shot through her as he tweaked her nipple. "Yes," she murmured. "Yes." His lips traveled across her cheek and he nibbled her earlobe; the sensation made her a little crazy. When she wriggled against him in a desperate attempt to get closer, he seemed to go crazy too.

He growled—*growled*—and shifted down, enveloping her throbbing nipple through the lace of her bra. Wet heat. Suction. Her thoughts flew, scattered to the four winds as pleasure trickled through her.

Mindless, boneless, swamped with need, she fiddled with the catch of his pants. But dang it...she couldn't get them undone. In her fumbling, her hand brushed against something hard and insistent and he muttered an imprecation. He was too beset to remember to apologize, which she found amusing.

She cradled him, gauging his length, his width, his girth.

And yes. He was magnificent. "Stone," she whispered as she tightened her hold. "You're so hard."

"Jesus, Lily. Don't do that."

"I can't help it. I want to feel you. Take your stupid pants off."

"They're not stupid," he snorted in a laugh, but he complied, sitting up to kick off his boots and slough his trousers off. As he hunted in his pack for something, she pulled her jeans off too.

He yanked off his shirt and came back to her, sealing their chests together. It was wonderful. His skin was warm and smooth, though she found a couple scars. She could rub against him all day.

But he had something else in mind.

After another scorching kiss, he pulled away. She started to complain until she realized it was to kiss his way down her body. As he suckled and sipped, he caressed her. She tingled wherever he touched her…and he touched her everywhere.

When he reached her belly, he glanced up and held her gaze as he slipped her panties off.

Her breath caught.

Oh God. Oh God.

He edged between her legs and spread her knees and buried his face.

She nearly screamed. The touch of his tongue on her clit sent shards of exquisite sensation through her. She was hard there, and aching. His laving soothed her, but stoked another fire. When he moaned how good she tasted, the sound rumbled through her, sending more delicious pings through to her core.

She probably shouldn't have buried her nails in his head and ridden his face as he ate her, consumed her, but she was wild, unleashed. Crazed as she never had been. It felt so good, and he was skilled. He seemed to know just how to touch, where to nip, when to lap.

The orgasm was a surprise. It leaped upon her like a jungle cat and gobbled her whole. Brilliant shimmers of exquisite colors exploded in her mind as wave upon wave of bliss claimed her.

But he didn't stop. No. Not this machine. He kept working her, tantalizing her, driving her higher and higher.

When her second climax hit, he seemed to sense it and, just as she dissolved, he shoved two thick fingers deep.

She tried to cry out. She tried to wail, but her voice was lost, along with her sanity, winging away into some far-off dimension.

Still, he didn't let up. He found that spot, that tiny spot hidden in her folds, where all her nerves joined and her being coalesced. He rubbed it, teased it, until she was shaking and quivering and boneless again.

He moved up her body and Lily was battered by conflicting waves of regret and anticipation. Regret that the ecstasy had stopped, though he still stroked her lightly, and anticipation because, as he rose, he gazed downward, aiming his fisted cock for heaven.

"Stone," she whispered, as he nudged her entrance. "Stone."

He was well named.

His erection was hard as a rock.

Jesus God. She was wet. Slick and hot and tight.

Stone squeezed his eyes shut as he worked the head of his cock into her. It was fucking heaven.

She was fucking heaven.

She'd been gorgeous, beautiful, amazing, writhing beneath him, coming again and again with hardly any prompting. The second time, she'd flooded him with her arousal and he'd known—*known*—she was ready. But he'd wanted to bring her to the brink one more time.

He wanted to make her come again.

He adjusted his position so he had a better angle, and drove home. She cried out and shivered around him, a maddening squeeze. Goddamn, she was amazing. She clasped his cock as she clasped his body, wrapping herself around him and holding on for dear life.

He doubted he had much patience, but he was determined to try and make this last. She made it hard on him, moaning and huffing and growling in his ear, murmuring evil little comments like, *"Yes, harder. Fuck me, Stone."*

There was only so much of that a man could take before he went absolutely apeshit wild.

He tightened his muscles and eased his cock in and out in a slow, salacious drag.

This, apparently, annoyed her. She glared up at him and snapped, "Faster. Faster."

And really, who was he to refuse a lady?

Bracing himself on his elbows, he increased his speed, wedging her legs farther apart with his knees and bending to suckle at her breast. He wished he'd removed her bra, but that ship had sailed. No way was he stopping to do it now. So he settled for teasing the pebble-hard tips through the lace—which, apparently, drove her insane.

She tried to wriggle and thrash, but he held her still, as he whipped in and out of her in a frenzy of passion, pummeling her, ravishing her, taking all he wanted, and more.

His fervor seemed to reignite hers. They wrestled against each other in a combat that had two victors. In concert, they raced toward perdition.

"Yes," she cried, sinking her fingers deep into the cheeks of his ass. A sharp thrill snaked through him as she tugged on a sensitive spot.

"Oh yeah," he muttered. "Yeah."

Unbelievably, she came again, and it was his undoing.

It began with small ripples and quickly swelled to hellish quakes. Each one snarled through his body, a mind-bending torment. His long, hard stokes dissolved to shorter, quicker, deeper thrusts. Faster and faster, like rapid fire, he took her. His cock swelled. His balls constricted. His muscles seized.

And fuck.

Everything exploded. His body, his heart, his soul. Something deep inside him released and he felt as though he was soaring, wheeling in the sky, dancing in the wind. It was the most incredible experience he'd ever had.

The most beautiful conflagration.

Even when it was over, sinuous sizzles coiled through him. He trembled as he hovered over her, gasping, struggling for balance. He stared down at her, this woman, this miracle. This creature who could never be his.

But this night was his.

This night, she was with him.

And the memory would be his for all time.

When he covered her mouth and kissed her with grief-stricken gratitude, she responded with a matching anguish that surprised him.

Perhaps they weren't so different after all.

Oh my.

Lily stared at Stone, his beautiful face transformed in bliss. Oh, that had been splendid. Better than she could ever have dreamed or hoped or wished for. Certainly far and above any experience she'd ever had. Ever.

But then, she'd never been so wildly attracted to a man.

She'd meant what she said. She'd never met anyone like him.

It wasn't just that he was a SEAL—what woman didn't fantasize about these modern warriors?—it was *him*. The way he made her *feel*.

He collapsed by her side and fiddled with something. It was a surprise to realize he was removing a condom. She hadn't even seen him put it on. And—to her mortification—she hadn't thought about protection herself. Thank God he had.

He buried it in the soft dirt, and then pulled her into his arms and held her as his breathing came back to normal. Oh heavens. She loved this too. Making love with him had been amazing, but this was…well, it was exquisite. She'd never felt as *safe* as she did in his arms.

She kissed the underside of his chin. It was speckled with fuzz, which she found fascinating. He responded by tucking his head and kissing her again. This time, the kiss was soft and sweet. He sighed, but he didn't speak.

They lay there for a long while, just soaking in each other's warmth and reveling in the gentle waves of afterglow. It was difficult for Lily to remain silent. She wanted to dance and sing and say something stupid like, *"Was it good for you?"* But she sensed he needed this time, this peace, and she didn't want to break the fragile spell winding between them.

When he finally spoke, it wasn't what she expected.

"Are you okay?"

Okay? She was fantastic. "I'm fine."

"I'm sorry…"

She wrenched out of his hold and glared at him. "Sorry? For what?"

He shot her with a repentant smile. "I shouldn't have been so rough."

The sound she made could have been a laugh. Or a snort. He'd been feral. Wild. Crazed. It had been awesome.

"Did I hurt you?"

"No. You didn't hurt me. You weren't too rough. It was…"

His muscles tensed as she searched for just the right word. But none of the words that came to mind seemed to adequately describe—

He came up on his elbow. "What? It was…what?"

Her eyes glowed. "Perfect."

"Perfect?" His face broke into a grin.

"Perfect." She caressed his cheek and thumbed his dimple. "One thing though?"

His brow rippled. "Um…yeah?"

"When can we do it again?"

He barked a laugh; it rang off the ring of rocks. Then he gathered her in his arms and pulled her back down. "Give me a minute to recharge."

"A minute?"

"With you?" He winked. "Yeah. A minute. But…"

"But, what?"

"It would help if you took off your bra."

She was quick to comply.

He didn't intend to fuck her again. Hell, he hadn't *intended* to fuck her the first time. But as they lay there on the hard ground, entangled, and he teased her soft skin, explored her supple breasts, and feasted on those button-hard nipples, Stone found it didn't take long to recharge at all.

On top of all that, he was very aware they didn't have much time. The chopper would probably be coming in at first light. Once they were picked up, once he was back with his platoon and she was returned to her father, they would never see each other again.

He wasn't sure why that realization lent desperation to his moves, but it did.

And as fan-fucking-tastic as the first time had been, the second was better, which blew his mind.

Hell, *she* blew his mind.

They kissed and touched each other playfully at first. A caress here, a nibble there. Her forays were shy, but as passion rose so did her boldness. When she took him in hand and fisted his cock, his breath stalled, but that was nothing to the sheer blinding lust that engulfed him when she scooted lower…and licked him.

Holy God.

Her mouth was hot and slick, her tongue mischievous, her suction mind-bending. She worked his cock like she was starved for it, craving a taste of his cum. Sucking and lapping and taking him deep.

At one point, he nearly lost control, but damn, he was glad he hadn't when she crawled on top of him and took him in.

He shouldn't have let her do that, but it felt so good, skin to skin. The folds of her channel were velvety smooth and slick and tight. Before he lost all control, he lifted her off and leaned over to find another condom. Goddamn, he should have left them closer.

It seemed to take forever to find one in his pack, but he ripped it open and slipped it on, ignoring the fact that his fingers shook.

"There." He lay back and grinned at her.

Her smile lit a fire in his belly.

The sight of her angling a leg over his torso and taking him in again was like a splash of kerosene on that fire. And fuck, it felt good.

She rode him then, like he was a bucking bronc. Up, down, around in torturous circles. He held her, tried to guide her movements with fingers buried in the flesh of her hips, but she would not be controlled.

She did as she liked, fucking him, pleasuring herself on his aching rod.

Her breasts were irresistible. He cupped them and tried to hold on as she moved, tweaking the nipples to urge her to higher and higher passion.

It was a slower climb to heaven this time, but no less powerful for the leisurely ascent. When she came, her body convulsed around him. The scintillating sensation of her helpless quivers and quakes made his vision dim.

With her orgasm, she became boneless and crumpled onto his chest. He rolled over, taking her with him, and without breaking their connection, began to thrust.

Ah. What a relief to control the movements, to take her masterfully, powerfully. To possess her completely.

Something deep within him coiled; his muscles quivered with the tension. He sucked in a breath, preparing for the onslaught of glory as tension mounted.

It rose to an unbearable height, lashing him with need, scalding him with an agonizing heat. Little skitters ran up and down his spine and settled at his core.

With a shudder, he broke. The orgasm screamed through him, buffeting him about, taking him and tossing him asunder.

It was a glorious asunder.

He'd never felt so emptied. So filled. So complete.

He remained there, poised over her, buried in her, reveling in the moment, in her.

She murmured something unintelligible and then her lashes fluttered closed.

God, she was beautiful.

But it was more than that.

There was something about her he couldn't put his finger on. A rightness, perhaps. When she was in his arms, he felt as though everything in the world fit right in place.

He wouldn't think on tomorrow. Couldn't. This moment was all there was. With him and Lily, connected. Everything was wonderful.

Wonderful. Yes.

Until he pulled out and removed the condom and realized…it had broken.

Shit.

Goddamn Garrett and his fucking *old* condoms.

"Lily?"

No response. He glanced down at her. Her eyes were closed. A tiny snore rumbled. She was asleep. Poor thing. This had been a hell of a day. He had no right to exhaust her all night.

He could tell her in the morning. He *would* tell her in the morning.

For now, he'd let her sleep.

"Lily," he said again, but softly, and only to himself. He kissed her brow and pulled her into his arms and arranged her head on his chest. Hopefully he was not too hard of a pillow.

He didn't feel hard at the moment.

At the moment, he felt like a limp noodle that had been thrown against the wall.

He was definitely knocked off balance.

These feelings swimming around in his head and in his heart were so new, he wasn't sure how to interpret them.

Or if he should.

All he knew was, come morning, he didn't want to let her go.

But he had to.

CHAPTER NINE

A rustling roused her. That and a sharp pain in her hip. Sleeping on the hard ground apparently didn't agree with her. Lily shifted and another ache rippled through her lower body, but this was a pleasurable one. A smile curled her lips as she recalled their adventures the previous night. Oh, how amazing had that been?

She'd loved having him over her, but she had really enjoyed riding him too. Stone was so large, she'd had to stretch her knees wide to encompass the girth of his hips…and that had allowed her to take him deep—

A shudder swept through her as she remembered the bliss, along with a humming curiosity. Would he want to do it again this morning? She opened her eyes and saw him gathering their things and organizing his backpack and her heart sank.

It was still dark, but a hint of light shone through the trees. The stark beauty of his face, the coiled power of his body, his height, the breadth of his shoulders… Though she'd seen it all, felt it all, experienced it all, his magnificence struck her anew.

Something in her chest pinged. Her throat locked. Apprehension, tangled with an unaccountable joy, sifted through her.

Oh dear.

Surely this feeling was not what she thought it was.

They'd known each other two days. Kissed a few times. Made love twice. Why did she have this sinking suspicion that if he walked out of her life today, she might die?

And why, for heaven's sake, was she wrapped in fear that he

might not feel the same?

She'd gone the length of her life without this man in it.

It had been dreary and dull, but she'd survived.

Perhaps she could ignore the fact that the sight of him, the thought of him, the knowledge of him, changed everything.

Or perhaps not.

Her attention snagged on his rippling muscles as he pulled on his body armor and cinched it up. She should have closed her eyes and pretended she was still asleep, but she couldn't look away. He noticed after a while that she was awake, and he sent her a tight smile.

A tight smile? Why did that make her mood plunge?

"Good morning." His voice was a gruff rumble, as though he'd worn it out calling her name the night before.

"G-good morning." It was an effort, forcing out the words. She sat up and worked her fingers through the tangles of her hair.

"How did you sleep?" He held out an energy bar. She took it, though her fingers were numb.

"Well." She ripped open the bar and took a bite. It tasted like cardboard. She hated this wall between them. This cool *politeness*. Where had it come from? "And you?"

"Fine. But I'm used to this." He shoved a few more things into his pack. "We should get ready to go. I want to be on the beach when the chopper arrives."

"Oh." Right. The chopper. Which would take them away. Was it wrong of her to want to stay? Just a little while longer? "Stone?"

He stilled, and then shot her a cold glance. No, not cold so much as…dispassionate. Hooded. Distant. "Yes?"

"Can we talk about…last night?"

He crossed his arms and looked at her.

Just looked. Waiting for her to speak. But she didn't know what to say. Silence hummed between them.

At long last, he muttered, "We shouldn't have."

Her pulse thrummed. Oh, hell no. She wasn't letting him off that easy. "But we did." And then, when he didn't respond, "Twice."

There was no need for him to glare at her. She glared right back.

"Lily—"

"Don't say it." She knew. She could tell from his tone, his expression, the tension in his stance. *It was over.* She didn't want to hear it. She leaped to her feet and began folding the blanket.

"Leave that."

She frowned at him and continued folding, though she didn't do a very good job because she could barely see. Fury blinded her.

They'd shared something amazing last night and now he was acting as though it had been a mistake. Apathy would have been better than that cold, impassive stare, that tinge of regret.

"Lily…"

"What?" She whirled on him, dropping the blanket on the ground, fists on her hips.

"I'm sorry. But we shouldn't have."

"Was I that bad?" It hadn't seemed like he'd hated it.

"No!" He sprang toward her, and then remembered himself and backed away again. "It was amazing. *You* were amazing. But…we shouldn't have done it."

"Why not?"

He raked his fingers through his hair—what there was of it. If he had hair, maybe his ears wouldn't poke out so much. A petty thought, but she felt at the moment she deserved at least one. His lips worked as he tried to find the words, the justification, the lame excuse. "For one thing, I'm on a mission…"

"And *I'm* the mission."

"Yes!"

"Well, you *did* your mission." He didn't laugh at her joke. Probably because it didn't sound like a joke, snarled as it was.

His lips tightened. His face went pale beneath his tan. "Goddamn it! It wasn't like that. You just don't understand. I don't *do* things like that. I never do."

The energy bar in her belly churned. It was not pleasant. "Really?" she snapped. "Is that why you carry condoms with you?"

He made a noise. Something between a growl and a grumble. "Those were a prank. Someone put them into my pack. And they weren't very—shit, Lily. We need to talk about that too."

"About what?"

"One of them…broke."

"Great." She threw up her hands.

"You're on birth control, right?" Why his question filled her with rage was a mystery. Or not.

How dare he make *that* the issue, rather than the real reasons for his retreat? And she knew the truth. The *real* reasons were either disinterest—that he had only used her to scratch an itch—or fear. Both options pissed her off.

"It hardly matters whether I'm on birth control or not, does it?"

His throat worked. "It matters very much."

"It's none of your business, so it doesn't matter."

"If you get pregnant, it *is* my business."

"Is it?"

Tension crackled as he stared at her. "All of this is beside the point." Oh dear. This soft, silky tone was even worse than the bellowing. "It was wrong of me to weaken. To…lead you on."

"Lead me on?" A cold wind blew through her.

A tangle of befuddlement and regret rippled over his features. "I'm a SEAL, Lily. The life, the mission is all there is for me."

She flinched as his meaning hit home.

"There can never be anything more between us."

Ah. There it was.

"Fine." She turned away and began moving things around. She wasn't cleaning or packing, she didn't have the wherewithal for that. Just moving things around so she looked busy and he wouldn't notice her tears.

"Lily…"

"I get it, Stone. Just drop it."

"I want you to understand. It isn't you—"

Her laugh was harsh. Incongruous. "Yes, yes. It isn't you. It's me. I know. I know."

"That's not what I mean." He whipped her around with a hard hand to her arm. He stilled when he saw the tears. His flinty façade wavered. "Don't cry, Lily."

"I'm not crying." She yanked away and rubbed at her cheeks.

"Shit, I'm fucking this up. I didn't mean to hurt you, Lily. It's just that I made a vow never to get involved. Never do to a woman what my dad did to my mom."

"Which was?"

"Leave her. I have a dangerous job. I go places. Do things. Sometimes, men don't come back."

"So you'll never have a meaningful relationship with someone— *ever*—because sometime, at some point in the future, you might not come back?"

"My mom was devastated."

"Thousands of soldiers, thousands of military wives deal with that fear every day. *Children* deal with that fear every day."

"It's not the same—"

"It is exactly the same thing." They glared at each other as silence sizzled. "Tell me one thing, Stone, and be honest. Did you even enjoy it a little?" She didn't mean for her voice to wobble.

He seemed to soften then. An infinitesimal crack in his battlements. "Ah, hell. Of course I did. It was incredible. It made me want—" He broke off and turned away, storming to the other side of the enclosure and then back again.

"It made you want...what?"

His expression was pained when he looked at her. "More. It made me want more. With you."

"But you won't allow it."

"I can't." He held out his hands in the age-old gesture of helplessness.

Bullshit.

Lily crossed her arms and turned up her nose. "You are a coward."

His jaw dropped. "What?"

"You heard me. A coward. I'm glad you don't want anything more to do with me, because as gorgeous as you are, and as funny and smart and, I'll be honest, good in bed...frankly, I don't have any use for cowardly men."

He blinked. "I... What?"

"Now, where is this helicopter going to land? I think we should get moving."

"But...wait."

She waggled her fingers at him, a dismissive gesture. "There's nothing more to talk about. It was fun while it lasted—as you said, probably just reaction to the adrenaline—but it's over. Wham, bam, thank you, Mr. SEAL. Good-bye." Oh, it hurt, her heart. It hurt like hell. And this blasé attitude was far from easy. But by God, he would not leave this debacle thinking he'd wounded her.

She couldn't bear it.

She just couldn't bear it.

Without looking at him, she picked up her rifle and her pack and started marching for the beach.

"Lily," he said, and her sure steps faltered. A faint hope flickered.

It died when he murmured, in a desolate tone, "The beach is the other way."

Well, fuck. That had not gone well.

Stone followed in Lily's wake, trying not to cringe as he ran through their conversation in his head. Well, okay, their fight. That's what it had been.

This was probably the real reason he didn't ever have relationships with women. Because he always screwed everything up.

He should have woken her with a kiss and thanked her for that lovely night and gently explained his vow and his reasons for it, instead of bleating it out like a sheep. No wonder her feelings had been hurt.

The sight of tears on her cheeks had killed him. Never in his life had he felt more inept than when seeing her cry.

But the real horror? The cold wave washing through his gut? When her expression had gone stony and her lips pursed and she said…

What had she said?

"You're a coward."

He shuddered.

Yeah. Pretty fucking heinous.

Though he had to admit, it was probably true.

Even that hadn't hurt as much as what she said next.

"I don't have any use for cowardly men."

He comforted himself with the fact she'd said he was gorgeous. And funny. Smart. Good in bed. He'd really liked that one.

But she had no use for him.

He shouldn't feel devastated. It was what he wanted.

Wasn't it?

To protect her from a danger no one could predict? To protect her from…the call?

The day the call had come about his father was burned on his brain. He'd never heard a woman wail the way his mother wailed. Never seen a human being *crumble*. He still woke up at night sometimes in the cold clutch of that memory.

The image of Lily getting such a call, screaming to the heavens and pounding her fist on the countertop, was untenable. The thought of Lily losing her bright spirit and slipping into the darkness raked his soul. When grief was too much to bear, sometimes people did desperate things.

Stone had been the one to find his mother three days later. He'd been a boy. Fifteen. He'd never seen so much blood; the bathroom was drenched in it. Thank God he'd come home from school early. Thank God he'd found her in time.

Thank God she'd been able to get the help she needed to deal with her anguish. But she had never been the same. Not really.

He would do anything, give anything, to protect Lily from that.

Because, damn it all to hell, he loved her.

Somehow she'd snuck in under all his defenses. Snuck in like a stealth warrior and buried her talons deep in his heart.

It was going to be hell walking away from her, but at least he had his memories of last night to keep him warm in the cold nights ahead.

It was for the best.

She'd move on. Find some guy she did have use for.

Marry him. Have babies.

Never get the call.

She deserved a better life than he could give her. Stone tried not to let that thought burn him alive.

He glanced down at her as they emerged from the trees onto the beach. The sun was just starting to rise and the soft light licked her features and glimmered off her hair.

So beautiful. So precious.

The best thing he could do for her was give her up. And as hard as it would be, it would be worth it.

Because she'd be happy. She'd be safe. And—

The bullet hit him with no warning, slamming into his chest with a bone-breaking smack. He flew back, dimly registering Lily's cry and the bellow of an approaching pirate.

Fuck! he railed at himself. He should have been paying more attention. His body armor had stopped the round, but pain snarled through his shoulder; his right arm was numb. He tried to grasp his weapon but couldn't close on it. Fear for Lily's safety whipped through him like a cold wind.

He looked over to where she had been and saw her backing into the woods.

Good girl, he thought. With any luck, they hadn't seen her. Or at the very least, he could buy her some time to escape. At any rate, she would need help.

With his left hand he pulled out the canister and flipped the lid, sending a plume of red smoke up into the air—red for distress. The extraction team should be out, watching for it, and they could whip in and save her.

As for him? He was helpless as a babe. He couldn't even reach his grenades.

Sand sprayed his face as a skinny, bedraggled pirate skidded to a halt over him, pointing an old AK-47 at him and screaming in Somali.

Stone had stared down the barrel of a rifle before, but he'd never been so certain that *this was it.*

This was the moment. This was the time he'd expected and prepared for since the day he'd joined up.

This was the day he was going to die.

His only regret was that Lily, sweet Lily, would witness it.

CHAPTER TEN

Horror curled through Lily as a shot rang out and Stone fell. It must have been pure instinct that sent her scrambling for the bushes, because her brain had simply stopped working.

She found herself hunkered low with her rifle held up, and no memory of moving at all.

The pirate, a man she recognized from the boat but hadn't seen since, ran down the beach toward Stone's prone form. Revulsion rose in her throat as he lifted his rifle and snarled something in a language she didn't understand. She could tell from his stance, from the angle of the weapon, he intended to shoot Stone in the head.

Oh no. Hell no.

The thought of losing him—like this—was beyond contemplation.

Though she'd never used a rifle before, though she'd never sighted one or pulled a trigger, she sucked in a breath and aimed. This weapon had misfired before. She hoped to God it wouldn't do so again.

Squeezing her eyes shut, she pulled the trigger.

The retort was deafening, or maybe that was the sound of her pulse pounding in her ears. The impact knocked her back as the butt slammed into her shoulder.

She scrabbled back up and peered out at the beach, every nerve humming.

A plume of red smoke obscured the scene—but then the wind shifted and it cleared. The pirate was on the sand, next to Stone. But the shot had been so deafening, Lily didn't know if she and the pirate had shot at the same time…and Stone was so still. Dreadfully still. She dropped her pack and the rifle and sprinted onto the beach.

Her heart clenched as she collapsed at Stone's side. His eyes were closed. He wasn't moving. With all his gear, it was impossible to check for a chest rise.

Terror settled like a cold cloud on her soul. "Stone!" she bellowed, shaking his shoulder. To her relief, his lashes fluttered, and then opened.

"Lily," he croaked. His lips tweaked.

"Oh, you'd better be okay," she muttered. "If you were hurt, I'd kill you."

For some reason, this made him laugh. He glanced over at the pirate. "You shot him?" he groaned as he sat up.

"I think so." She hadn't looked. Kind of didn't want to know. She'd never shot a person before. "I closed my eyes."

He snorted. "You closed your eyes?"

"Mmm hmm."

He leaned over and checked the pirate's face. "Oh, yeah. You got him." But when she moved to check for herself, he held her back. "You…don't want to see."

Probably not.

"Do you think he was alone?" she asked, scanning the beach. She saw nothing. Nothing but the gently shushing waves, the palms waving in the breeze, and the shimmer of a deserted beach reaching into the distance.

"Probably a lone scout," Stone said. "I don't see anyone else." Still, he reached for his rifle and held it at the ready.

Reaction set in and Lily shivered. Her pulse still throbbed in her temple and her skin was clammy. The gush of relief that he wasn't hurt made her dizzy. "Oh, Stone, I was so scared. Normally I would never shoot someone—"

"Normally?" He chuckled.

"But he was going to hurt you."

"Yes. He was. Thank you very much for saving me."

"Well," she said with a huff, a sudden heat crawling up her cheeks. "You saved me. More than once."

The wind changed and the cloud of smoke blew back over them. Lily waved her hand in front of her face and coughed. "What is that?"

"A marker. So the chopper can find us."

And even as he said it, she heard a distant, rhythmic thrum.

Was it wrong to be so swamped with regret? That this was over? That soon, they could no longer be together? That she would probably never see him again?

She didn't think. Didn't bother to consider her actions. She took his face in her hands and kissed him. He sifted his fingers through her hair and held her there as he returned the kiss.

"I understand," she said as she lifted her head. "I understand why you feel so strongly about keeping yourself detached."

"Lily—"

She didn't allow him to interrupt. This needed to be said. "But Stone, if you ever change your mind, if you ever decide you do want something more, please think of me. Find me. I would take it all, I would take anything…for you."

His eyes glimmered as he stared at her. His lips worked, but he said nothing.

"Although," she said, "I cannot imagine anything worse than watching you be gunned down on a beach."

"That was nothing," he muttered. "A scratch."

"It was a bullet." She touched the lump of metal nested in his vest, so close to his heart.

He winced.

"Does it hurt?"

"Damn right it hurts."

"But you're wearing armor."

"It still hurts like hell."

She smacked his shoulder.

"Ow." He frowned. "What was that for?"

"You should have told me that when *I* was wearing it. Here I thought I was all safe and everything."

"You were safe." He glanced up at the chopper coming in to land just down the beach. Sand and water sprayed them. "You *are* safe. I would never let anything happen to you. Lily…" His throat worked.

"Yes, Stone?"

"I… I would die if anything happened to you."

She wondered at that pause, but only for a moment. There was hardly any time left. She didn't waste a second.

She kissed him again.

That there was a woman—a hostage, no less—kissing Stone as the Zipperhead Twins jogged down the ramp of the Chinook was not lost on them. Stone saw it in their shit-eating grins. Garrett opened his mouth to say something as he helped Stone to his feet and wrapped an arm around him, but before he could say anything, Stone growled at him to shut up.

Luke snorted and clapped him on the chest. Stone flinched.

"Be careful!" Lily barked.

Garrett fixed her with a bemused look. "Ma'am?"

Lily set her fists on her hips. Her glower was terrifying. Also, adorable. "He's been shot. Do be careful."

"Have you been shot, Stone?" Luke asked.

Garrett smirked as he led Stone to the chopper. Luke followed with Lily, so hopefully she didn't hear his murmured, "Did widdle Ryder get shot by a mean bullet?"

"Fuck off, Garrett."

"Who's Ryder?"

Shit. Stone nearly groaned aloud. She had heard. "I'm Ryder," he said.

Her eyes widened. "*Ryder?*"

"Ryder Maddox, ma'am," Luke said. His expression made his meaning clear. *You should know the name of the man whose face you were just sucking on.*

Lily frowned. "But you said your name was Stone."

"I said people call me Stone." And hell. He should have told her his real name. At least before making love…

"Because he's stone cold." Yeah. He should smack Garrett.

Stone forced a smile. "And hard. A terrible pillow." This he said for her ears alone, but the others heard. They hooted with laughter. Lily assaulted them with a scorching rain of fire. Or it could have been a glare. Either way, they both cringed.

They were smart, those two. They knew when to cringe.

"You want to get into the chopper, ma'am?" Luke asked with only a tiny hint of sarcasm. "We would very much like to rescue you."

The look she sent him would freeze ice. But she did climb in, slapping away Luke's hands when he tried to help.

Stone clambered into the Chinook, nodded to the other troops, who'd come along as backup, and dropped into his seat with an *oof.* Lily sat next to him and he fit a headset on her. It took a while because his grip was iffy. The nerves on his right side were still screaming.

Luke bounded aboard and gave the signal to take off. He and Garrett popped on their headsets too. The headsets were necessary for conversations in the loud chopper, but the problem was, everyone heard everything. There was no privacy. No whispered conversations. No chance to talk to her without these two yahoos— and every man aboard—hearing every word. So Stone didn't speak. They all sat silently, glaring at each other as the chopper rose, turned, and skimmed over the sparkling sea.

"Where's your brain bucket?" Luke asked.

"Lost it," Stone grumbled. "Along with coms. The first night."

"Yeah. That was a cluster—" Garrett glanced at Lily and choked on the words. He cleared his throat and finished with a lame, "Charlie Foxtrot."

"No shit," Luke muttered.

A clusterfuck for sure. It was a relief to be out. A relief to know Lily was safe. But Stone burned to know more. He wasn't used to being in the dark. He shot a sharp glance at Garrett and Luke. "And the team? Everyone safe?"

It was disconcerting the way they didn't answer. The way they met each other's gazes and pressed their lips together.

Stone's heart lurched. "Drake?"

Garrett looked away. Luke swallowed. "We lost Zack."

Goose bumps prickled his nape. "I know that. What about Drake?"

"Tate took a hit. And Mason got a little dinged up. But they're okay."

Why weren't they answering him?

Well, hell. He knew why. Because the answer was bad. Real bad. His blood went cold. "What. About. Drake?"

He probably shouldn't have snarled. There was a lady present. But these two fuckwads were getting on his last nerve. If anything had happened to Drake, he didn't know what he would do. How would his mom take it? Christ. It would kill her. Drake was her baby, her only son, her golden boy. Her—

Lily set her hand on his and squeezed. Garrett and Luke didn't miss that either. But at least they didn't smirk or make some lame comment that might earn them a fist in the kisser. He was not in the mood for lame comments at the moment.

Garrett's lashes flickered. "We, ah, don't know what has happened to Drake."

"You don't know?" Pain rose in Stone's chest, squeezing his oxygen supply off. His head went light.

"Last report we had, he and one of the hostages were headed up the beach for the extraction point. He'd been hit in the leg and was going slow. And then…" Garrett glanced at Luke.

"And then…?"

"Coms cut out."

Hell.

Goddamn coms.

"He missed the pick-up."

"And his GPS?"

"Shows he's still on the other island. He hasn't moved for several hours."

Shit.

"Are we going in?" Why did he need to ask? Of course they were going in. "Is a team prepared?"

Luke made a face. "The brass has been trying to negotiate with the pirates."

Goddamn brass. They should just let them go in and do their jobs. Why the fuck were they negotiating? Drake was still in enemy territory. He clenched his jaw.

Lily's hold on his hand tightened. "It'll be okay," she whispered.

Yeah. For her it would be—and thank God for that.

But for him, the outcome was unclear.

Drake was in danger. For all Stone knew, he could be dead.

By the time the chopper landed on the deck of the *USS Sierra Nevada*, Stone was in a wad. He whipped off his headset and grabbed Lily's arm, helping her off the craft and guiding her belowdecks to the war room without a word.

He was torn. On the one hand, their precious time together was running out and he wanted nothing more than to hold her, maybe kiss her again. Though with his job, they couldn't be together the way she wanted, the way she deserved, at the very least he should offer her a sweet farewell—something that would make her remember him long after they'd parted. But he was incapable of that.

Because—on the other hand—he churned with agitation to finish this mission. His warrior instincts were on high alert. He needed to find Brandywine and Harper and give them a debrief…and fucking convince them to go in for an extraction *now*. SEALs did not leave a man behind. Ever.

That this man was *Drake* ate at him. Bile churned in his belly.

The pirates had lost most of their hostages and, if the counts he'd gotten from Garrett were correct, a lot of their men. Men who'd lost a lot tended to be desperate. The longer Drake was in the fire, the more dangerous the situation could become.

If he had to choose one thing to focus on, it had to be the mission. Still, he towed Lily along because the brass would want to debrief her as well.

And he couldn't bear to let her go. Not just yet.

He burst into the war room and came to an abrupt halt. Lily, who was following close behind, bumped into him with an *eep*.

Harper and Brandywine and another man were scouring the sat maps on the table. A cluster of men in black suits in the corner came to attention when they saw him. Once they determined he was not a threat, they relaxed.

Harper glanced up and grimaced. "You look like hell, Maddox."

"Thank you, sir."

The lieutenant broke into a grin. "But I'm glad to see you alive."

"Yeah." Stone rubbed at the ache in his chest. "Glad to be alive. But sir, we need to go back in—"

Harper held up a hand. "Stone, you're preaching to the choir. We've already got things in motion."

In motion? In fucking motion? They needed to go…*now*. Fly to the fucking X. Drop in. Waste these fuckers and pull Drake out. "Sir—"

The third man, who seemed somewhat familiar—but out of place in a navy-issued jumpsuit—stepped forward. He was a tall, slender man with closely cropped black hair, sporting a sprinkling of silver at the temples. His features were tense and drawn. With a hit to the gut, Stone realized who he was. His skin prickled.

"They said you had my daughter," the senator said in a gruff voice. "Where is she?"

"Daddy?" Lily peeped out from behind him and then rushed into the room, barreling into her father's arms.

"Oh. Thank God," the senator gushed as he wrapped her in a crushing hug.

It was natural for her to cry, Stone supposed. He didn't know why it tore him up to hear her sobs. Maybe the fact that now she was safe—in her father's arms—and it was definitely over. Whatever *it* was.

She didn't *belong* to him anymore. If she ever had.

Fuck. He hated this.

He attempted to push the bleakness away. Stiffening his spine, he stormed over to the table and stared at the maps, quickly analyzing the plan of attack.

"Wilson was the one asking us to hold back," Brandywine murmured as Stone studied the op. "Now that his daughter is safe, we're going in full bore."

"We'll be taking three teams, air and marine assault," Harper added. "No need for surprise. We're shooting for sheer intimidation."

Stone nodded. "I want to go."

Harper studied him. Stone knew he looked like hell. He didn't care. When the lieutenant's attention narrowed in on the bullet wedged in his vest, he knew what he'd say. "You've been shot."

"It's nothing."

"You need to get to medical."

"Bullshit. There's no time for that."

"You've been fucking shot."

"It's nothing."

"Goddamn it, Maddox—" Harper choked on the words. His face went beet red. "Um, sorry, ma'am," he said.

Stone turned to find Lily at his side. Oh, he'd known she was there. He'd *felt* her approach. She set her hand on his arm. Her touch burned him. "You aren't going back in?" Her lip trembled. "You just got safe."

He set his teeth. "I have to, Lily. It's my job."

Her haunted expression made his chest hurt. Even more. "But Stone, can't someone else go?"

He put his hands on her slight shoulders, willing her to understand. "Sure they can. But Drake is a member of my team. This is my mission...and I know the lay of the land. I have to go."

"But Stone..."

His grip tightened. Damn. This was harder than he'd expected, but it had to be said. She needed to understand. Maybe now she would. "This is exactly what I meant, Lily. This is what I was talking about. This is what I do. When there's danger, I rush in."

Tears welled in her eyes. The sight burned him to a crisp. Her lip wobbled. She reached up to cup his cheek. "I don't want you to go." A whisper. A sigh.

He kissed her forehead—without thinking, but his brain wasn't working very well anyway. He couldn't help but notice the sharp shift in energy around them. Most specifically, her father's bristle. And Harper's. And Brandywine's.

Typically, SEALs didn't kiss their targets.

In front of their targets' fathers.

But they could bristle all they wanted. This was between him and Lily. Suddenly, he didn't give a damn who saw, who knew, or who cared. All that mattered was her. Her understanding. Her peace. And, in a very real way, just her.

"I have to go, baby. I just have to."

The senator made a strangled sound at the endearment and stepped forward, crossing his arms. Not a good sign. "And you are?" The question was clipped and sharp. Stone read between the lines. What he really meant was: *Who the* fuck *are you? And get your hands off my daughter.*

"Daddy." Lily frowned at her father as she stepped between the two men. "This is Ryder Maddox, but people call him Stone. He saved me."

The senator was not mollified. "I gathered as much." He gave Stone a scorching once-over and his lips curled a little bit.

"Daddy, you don't understand. He *saved my life*. A man had a gun to my head and *he* saved me."

The senator paled as he stared at his daughter. His Adam's apple worked. When his gaze shot to Stone's, he met it. He owed the man that much. Besides, he never backed down from a challenge. He was *not* a coward. Even if Lily thought him one. "Sir."

It took a while for the senator to decide what to do. Apparently the choices were to order Stone hung from the yardarms for kissing his daughter, or offer his hand. It was a relief when he thrust out his hand.

Shit, he had a firm handshake for a pencil pusher.

"Thank you for keeping my daughter safe," he muttered grudgingly.

"My pleasure, sir." Stone winced as the words slipped out. It had been his pleasure. In more ways than one. In more ways than *Daddy* needed to know about.

Harper cleared his throat. "We should get moving, Maddox. If you want to do a ride along, you're going to need fresh gear."

Stone nodded. Body armor wasn't guaranteed to stop endless hits. He needed to collect new ballistic plates, get fresh ammo, and restock his kit. He forced a soothing smile at Lily, but judging from her reaction it was not as comforting as he hoped. "Gotta go, Lily," he said.

Was this it? Was this the last time he would see her? The last words he'd ever speak to her?

Probably.

He wished he could wrangle up something memorable. Or romantic. Or clever. But he couldn't. He couldn't wade through the murk of his desolation to find the words.

She smiled back. It was sad and sweet. "Be safe," she whispered. This time, she kissed him. And not on the forehead. Silence settled in the room as the kiss, their final farewell, dragged on. Stone savored every second.

"Ahem." Fucking Harper.

Stone lifted his head and gazed down at her, memorizing her face, her scent, this moment, although he already had.

She patted him on the chest. "I'll be here when you get back," she said.

The senator issued a snort. "Absolutely not, young lady. We're leaving immediately. We have a jet standing by."

Stone's heart dropped. He'd known. He'd known this was it, but he'd really secretly hoped she'd still be here when he got back. He'd thought he could do it. He'd thought he could say a casual good-bye and walk away from her forever. But now that the time was here...

Maybe he *was* a coward.

Because he didn't think he could face life without her.

"Come along, Lily." The senator took her arm and tried to tug her from the room.

She steeled herself and didn't budge. Then Lily shot a look at her father, one Stone had never seen before. Or maybe he had. She had a flair for intractable looks—this one was fierce. She set her jaw in a stubborn line, opened her mouth, and said, "No."

Just *no.*

Her father gaped at her. "What did you just say?"

"No. We're staying until everyone comes out safe."

"Lily. Darling. I need to get you home. Your mother is beside herself."

"Call her and tell her I'm okay. But I'm not leaving." She crossed her arms over her chest. "Not. Yet."

"But—"

Her eyes blazed. The sight filled Stone with pride...and perhaps a flicker of fear. As tiny as she was, she was truly daunting when she wanted to be. "This is not a negotiation."

The senator paled. His eyes narrowed. His gaze shot to Stone and back to his daughter. "You never told me no before." It sounded like a complaint.

She patted his hand. "I'm sorry, Daddy, but I must insist. I won't rest at all until I know everyone is off that island."

The senator seemed to deflate as he blew out a breath. "Okay. Okay. I guess. I'll go call your mother..." He tromped over to the corner, where his security detail waited, and commandeered a sat phone.

Lily turned to Stone and grinned. "I learned that from you," she whispered.

"What?"

"Being all adamant. You're good at it."

He couldn't help it. He kissed her forehead. Her nose. Her lips.

He could have kissed her forever, but Harper cleared his throat again, reminding Stone that he needed to move. But hell, it was hard saying the words. "I have to go."

Her smile dimmed. "Will you be gone long?"

"As long as it takes."

Her chin tipped up. She nodded. A light, imbued with meaning, flared in her eye. "I'll wait. As long as it takes."

And somehow, they both knew she wasn't talking about the mission.

CHAPTER ELEVEN

Shit on a Shingle, Lily decided, was a terrible thing to do to America's fighting men. She poked at the grayish mound on her tray with a tin fork. She'd thought the MREs were hideous, but this far surpassed the dreaded meatloaf in sheer yuckiosity.

The *something-like-eggs* she'd had for breakfast had been little better. She liked to think she wasn't spoiled, but maybe she was. At the very least, soldiers deserved a massive raise, perhaps hazard pay, for eating this.

She glanced at the men seated at the surrounding tables. They didn't seem to mind the food. They shoveled it in as though it were manna from heaven.

Maybe it was her. Maybe her stomach was churning too much to truly enjoy the delights of the mess hall. Although, in truth, the place was aptly named.

Despite the gastronomic torture, she was so glad she'd insisted on staying. Because once Stone left, and after the commanders debriefed her—asking incessant questions—she'd finally been able to ask a few of her own. She had discovered, to her horror, that the hostage who had yet to be rescued was Brandy.

Now worry swamped her. Worry for both of them—her friend and her man. And yes, that was how she thought of him. He was *hers*.

He could make up all the stupid excuses he wanted, but she wasn't going to let him go. He was a fighter, a warrior.

Well, so was she.

Her new mantra? *What would be...would be what she made it.*

96

The only way she would allow this to end would be because he didn't want her. And if that was the case, by God, she'd make him admit it.

She peeped at the clock on the wall and frowned. He'd been gone far too long—much longer than it should have taken to zip over to the island and pick up a couple hostages. To make things worse, when she asked anyone what was going on, they all pressed their lips together and murmured it was classified.

As if she would *tell* anyone.

Her father kept urging her to leave as well, which she was not going to do.

He'd finally gotten the message—that his daughter was no longer a compliant creature who would meekly follow orders—and he'd gone off to tour the ship with one of the officers. They were all delighted to have a senator on board.

Or maybe not delighted, but they were good at pretending. Lily suspected the tour was just a ruse to keep him occupied. Her father, like most men, enjoyed large mechanical things with guns attached, so he'd happily gone along.

Which left Lily alone, surrounded in the chow hall by sailors and SEALs who wouldn't talk to her, and her security team, which had reattached to her like remoras.

Alone. With nothing to do.

Nothing but poke at her Shit on a Shingle and worry. And fret. And think.

Naturally, her thoughts gravitated to the night she and Stone had spent together in each other's arms. She relived every touch, every kiss. Despite Stone's conviction that once she was safe, her fascination with him would fade, she felt the opposite.

Her feelings for him solidified, along with her certitude.

He was the one for her.

She would take him any way she could—even on his terms.

The only fly in the ointment was the possibility that he hadn't been talking about *her* fascination waning when everything was back to normal. Maybe he'd been talking about *his*.

Guys like Stone probably fended off lovelorn women all the time. And Lily was nothing special. She was…just who she was. The likelihood that a man like him, with his convictions, would renounce his vow for someone like her was dismal.

She wouldn't know until he got back. Until everyone was safe. Until they could speak privately about all this.

And even if he told her what she feared most hearing—that *yeah, it had been great, but it was over*—she wanted, needed to know.

She couldn't rest until—

She stilled as a hum of energy rose around her; the hairs on the back of her neck stood up. A movement in the corner of her eye captured her attention and she turned toward the hatch just as Stone stepped through. Her heart lurched, then leapt, skipping in a manic tattoo.

He was back.

He was safe.

She drank in the sight of him. He was so handsome, so stalwart and brave. And grubby. His face was covered in goo again.

He hadn't even stopped to clean up. He'd come straight for her.

Or food.

He could have come straight for food...

She stood, stared at him. "Stone." Her lips formed the words, but they remained unspoken. She tried to read him. As always, his expression was inscrutable, but his attention was fixed on her and not the food.

Which was promising.

He took a step toward her, his features hard, unyielding. The energy between them sizzled. She despaired for a moment that he might not speak at all, and then...he broke.

"Lily." Her name wrenched from his lips. He opened his arms.

She ran to him, ignoring the hard juts of his armor and weapons and the tools on his belt. She clung, holding on to him for dear life. "You're safe."

"Of course I'm safe," he muttered. "Everyone is safe." Bone-deep relief tinged his tone.

"Drake?"

"In med bay."

"And Brandy?"

His brow wrinkled. "Brandy?"

"The other hostage?"

"Ah. Brandywine's daughter. Yes. She's safe too." He tucked a curl behind her ear. "She wants to see you."

Of course she did. But not yet. Not yet.

Lily traced the curve of Stone's jaw. Just seeing him was not enough. She needed a touch. The bristles of his beard scraped against her skin; it was very reassuring. As was the warm light simmering in his beautiful gray eyes.

"You waited." His voice broke on the words.

"I told you I would."

"I know you did. But I thought… I expected…"

"That I would run?" She met his eye. "I'm no coward."

He flushed as she referred to her earlier accusation. Then his jaw went hard. His throat worked. "I'm no coward either. Lily…"

When he didn't finish the thought, she decided it might be prudent to prompt him. "Yes?"

"Ah, Lily…if you want to…explore this… I mean… I'd be…well…"

For a man who wasn't a coward, he certainly had a difficult time making a declaration. So she stopped him. She set her palm on his cheek. "Me too, Stone." She went up on her toes and kissed him. "Whatever you want. Wherever this takes us."

He stilled. "Wherever?"

"Anywhere." In truth, she would go to the moon if he asked.

His lashes flickered. "I'm based in San Diego. I don't get to DC very often…"

She laughed. "I live in Seattle."

He gaped at her. "Really?"

"Yes."

"My mother lives in Seattle. I have a place there. I visit whenever I have leave."

"Well, there you go. Would you…like to…" Oh lordy. Now she was the one struggling with words.

"Would I like to what?" His voice was a low thrum. She liked the way he nuzzled closer. She liked everything about him. His breadth, his heat, his scent. More than liked. She craved him. Loved him.

She swallowed heavily. She'd never asked a man out before. Her nerves fizzled and popped. She steeled her spine. "Would you like to have a date…the next time you're in town?" Swamped with a sudden shyness, she dropped her gaze.

He tipped it back up. "Lily Wilson?"

"Yes, Stone Maddox?"

"I would very much like to have a date the next time I'm in town.

In fact, I must insist."

And then he yanked her into his arms and kissed her. Kissed her hard.

All the men in the chow hall cheered and hooted.

Except, of course, for the men in black suits and sunglasses, who talked into their wrists.

Book Two:

DRAKE

CHAPTER ONE

Panicked shouts echoed across the deck of the *Avonturier*. Brandy's blood curdled; she leaped to her feet and stared at the two boats jouncing on the waves, racing toward their cruise ship. Her heart thudded in her throat. *Shit*. In the Indian Ocean, off the coast of Somalia, it could mean only one thing.

Pirates.

She shot a look at Lily and her stomach clenched. As a field nurse, Brandy had seen plenty of action, but her friend Lily was totally inexperienced. A tourist in every sense of the word. She had a pie-in-the-sky sense of optimism that frequently got her in trouble.

It was up to Brandy to keep her safe. God knew none of the other passengers on this aid trip would be any help at all. Nancy was a flibbertigibbet and both Michael and Pierre liked to pose as real men.

"Quickly," Captain Garnier barked. "You must go below. Now."

All of the passengers sprang up from the table where they'd been enjoying a lovely alfresco luncheon to gape at him. The spindly table lurched, sending water goblets tumbling.

"Go. Now," the captain bellowed as they hesitated. "There's a hidden cubby in the storage hold. It should be large enough for all of you."

Brandy did as he commanded; she got all the way to the lower deck before she realized Lily wasn't behind her.

Shit.

She raced back up the stairs. Damn it all anyway. She and Lily had been roommates in college, and friends ever since. She loved her to death, but honestly. As the only daughter of a famous politician, Lily had lived a very sheltered life. In Brandy's experience, sheltered lives made people street stupid. Or, in this case, boat stupid.

By the time she reached the top deck, she could hear gunfire. Her chest tightened. God, she couldn't stand it if anything happened to Lily. Aside from that, if it did, the senator would kill her. This whole junket had been Brandy's idea. Go to Ethiopia and save the children. It had seemed like a good idea. Until now.

She pushed through the hatch just as a bullet zinged over her head, burrowing into the bulkhead with a howling sizzle. Pierre barreled past her with Lily on his heels. She collided with Brandy at the top of the stairs.

Yanking Lily inside, she slammed the heavy door. "Where the hell have you been?"

Lily sniffed. "Collecting Pierre. He wanted to watch."

Brandy caught her arm and dragged her down the stairs. "Heaven protect us from innocents and devils," she muttered.

"What's that supposed to mean?"

"Nothing. What were you thinking? Going after Pierre? You need to take care of your own ass. For pity sake, Lily, those were real bullets out there. A bullet doesn't care who your father is. Understand? And when bullets are flying, anyone can get shot. Trust me. I've patched up more than one bystander who took a stray."

"Well, I didn't get shot." And then, "Where are we going?"

"Into the hold." They rounded the final landing and emerged into a large space packed with crates and boxes. The others were being ushered by a crewmember into a hidey hole at one end.

"It smells down here."

Brandy blew out a sigh. "Get used to it, Lil. We could be here for a while. The pirates don't just go away. They stay. They follow you. They continue attacking until you outrun them or until help comes." She stopped and pinned Lily with a dark glower. "We're in real danger here. People die in situations like this. They get taken prisoner. Held as hostages. For years sometimes."

Finally. Finally she got through. Lily paled. She quit resisting. Brandy hurried after her into the cubbyhole. Once they were settled, she closed the door with a jerk.

The metal clang should have made her feel better. Made her feel safer.

But it didn't.

For the next few hours, the sounds of the attack echoed through the bowels of the boat to their hiding place. Rapid fire, shouts, even the impact of what felt like a torpedo. Brandy was certain the pirates would sink the ship rather than let them go.

Fear clawed at her gut. As she huddled, she plotted how to get Lily to safety if the ship started taking on water, but she didn't share her fears.

The others holed up with them were no help. Nancy sat there hugging her knees and whimpering. Michael sweated profusely, making the closed space smell of man-stank and Pierre kept cracking his knuckles as though, if the pirates found them, he would leap to their defense…or something.

With any luck Garnier could outrun the bastards until help arrived. These waters were speckled with fleets that regularly came to the aid of ships under attack, but the waters were vast.

A pity they didn't have any luck. No luck at all. A massive impact slammed into the stern on the starboard side…and the engine shuddered to a stop. Brandy's blood turned to ice. What followed was something of a panicked blur. They heard the pirates board. Gunfire and shouts and then the sounds of pillaging in the hold—right outside their door.

Everyone held their breath. Nancy even stopped whimpering, but her eyes were wide. Brandy nearly fainted when the pirates left the hold, but sometime in the night they returned. This time they did not bother with the pillaging. They came straight for their hideaway.

The cubby was locked from the inside, but only by a bolt. To Brandy's horror, the door jiggled. Everyone leaned back, as though that could save them from this looming threat.

It did not.

The pirates made short work of the flimsy barrier, wrenching the door open, and Brandy found herself staring through the weak beam of a flashlight at a ragtag group of skinny men holding Kalashnikovs. She swallowed heavily. As automatic rifles went, they were notoriously unreliable. But a bullet was a bullet.

Slowly she raised her hands, urging the others to do so as well.
They all did.

All but Lily. Who smiled at the pirates.

Smiled.

Oh, God help them all.

* * *

"Whadda we got?" Drake Ronan asked as he ducked through the
hatch and into the ship's narrow corridor. He had to move fast to
keep up with Ryder and the rest of the guys on his squad. None of
them—not one of them—waited for anyone.

"It's a hostage situation," Ryder tossed over his shoulder as he
hustled toward the briefing room. They'd gotten the call for this
mission in the middle of a training op and they'd had to chopper in.
They knew they were late. Probably the last squad to arrive. It
sucked, because this was Drake's first mission with this SEAL
team—his dream team—and he really wanted to impress. He was
determined to show everyone he had what it took to serve with this
elite company.

SEAL teams had a tendency to form tight bonds—necessary
when working in high-stress and dangerous situations—but it kind of
made it a bitch for the new guy to break in. Especially when his
squad leader didn't want him.

He hoped to prove Ryder wrong.

Maybe he shouldn't have pushed to be assigned with Ryder, but
shit, when he'd saved the admiral from a terrorist attack, the brass
had offered him his choice of assignments.

This was the team he wanted. The squad he needed. Fuck, this was
why he'd become a SEAL. To work with Ryder.

If Ryder didn't like it, he could just suck it.

Garrett bumped into him as they both tried to pass through the
same hatch and then he glared at Drake as though it were his fault.

Awesome.

No doubt Ryder had prepped the squad to give the new kid the
business.

So Drake shot Garrett a grin. A shit-eating grin.

Yeah. Kill 'em with kindness.

At the next hatch, Luke bumped into him. Figured. Garrett and

Luke were two peas in a pod. At the third hatch, when Zack did the same, it got old. So Drake tripped the fucker. Zack went plowing into Mason, who whirled around and frowned at him.

When Ryder turned around and glowered at *all* of them, Drake fixed an innocent look on his face. Whistled even.

"Come on, guys. Stay focused," he snapped. Ryder snapped a lot. Always had. He was a surly fuck sometimes. "This is a major op. A JTF. Best behavior."

"Aye, aye," they all chorused. They all knew the drill. When working on a joint task force there was one rule and one rule only. Impress the hell out of the other teams.

Ryder shot another frown around the cadre, just for good measure, pinning each member of his team with his displeasure. He pinned the most on Drake. Then again, he always had. Ever since they were kids.

Proving himself to Ryder was damn near impossible, but he would. Or die trying.

When they filed into the war room, all the other squads were assembled, so Lieutenant Harper lit right into the briefing, quickly going over the details of the incident. A ship, carrying aid workers headed for Ethiopia, had been taken by pirates. They had hostages. As Harper spoke, Drake glanced at the man to the CO's left and flinched.

Fuck.

Commander Brandywine.

Of all people.

Fuckity fuck fuck fuck.

He tried to make himself smaller, but it was too late. The commander saw him; his eyes narrowed.

Drake remembered Brandywine from his BUD/S training. The guy was a fucking legend. Also, he hated Drake's guts. Most likely because he'd been the one to drag Drake home after his company's Hall of Fame liberty—which had been dubbed, by many, as the infamous Hall of *Shame* liberty. For graduating with perfect marks, his team had earned a special unescorted leave. They'd torn up the fucking town.

Brandywine had been the one to collect them at the police station and drag their asses back to base; his opinion of Drake was not stellar.

It might have had something to do with the fact that Drake had barfed on his boots.

Brandywine's eyes narrowed, but he didn't say anything—like *get out*. Instead, he crossed his arms and fixed his attention on Harper waiting for his turn to speak as the lieutenant gave a preliminary overview of the operation. And when he did speak, Drake's gut clenched.

He'd wondered why someone of Brandywine's rank was here, overseeing this mission. The reason was a heartbreaker.

His daughter, Susan, was one of the hostages.

Drake stared at the slide on the screen, the picture of a smiling girl with nut-colored pigtails, a raft of freckles over her nose, a crooked smile…and braces.

"Shit," he murmured before he could stop himself. "Is she seven?"

Ryder gored him with an elbow and he *oofed*.

The commander sent him a cold look. His voice was rough when he responded. "This is the only photo I have of her. The last one her mother sent me. She is…older now." His throat worked as he scanned the company. "If you boys could bring my daughter home safely, I would be very appreciative." With that, the commander left the room and the tension drained from Drake's body.

Harper waited for the hatch to close on the war room before he continued. "I didn't want to stress this in front of him, but you all need to be aware. This is not your typical pirate crew. For most of these bastards, this is just a business. The crews try very hard to keep their hostages safe and in good health. They are respectful of women. These guys… Well, they've already killed one hostage. Needless to say, time is of the essence. Team medics, be sure your bags are stocked. We have no idea what we'll find."

The briefing continued, going over the assignments, the details of the drops and the extraction points. Harper flicked back through the slides to a map of the area, pointing out the island where the hostages were being held and the island to the south that would serve as a secondary extraction site if needed. Most such rescues took place aboard ship, but because these idiots had damaged the ship during their attack, they'd had to evacuate to an island in an archipelago off the coast of Somalia.

It pretty much seemed like your standard rescue op. Drop in, clear the area, take out the hostiles and transport the hostages—both passengers and crew—to safety. He'd done at least ten like this. Drake checked his watch. Couple hours, tops.

The only downer was that their squad would be away from the heavy action, clearing a village to the north when intel had all the hostages being held in the south. But hey, a mission was a mission.

The briefing ended and the men all bustled out of the room and back to their assigned bunks to assemble their gear. The squad was silent as everyone prepared their packs and checked their weapons. They'd all done this a thousand times, so no chatter was required.

Drake dropped his heavy vest on the bed and Ryder frowned. "Wear it," he clipped. "These pirates have already killed a couple crew members and one of the hostages. They won't balk at shooting a SEAL."

Drake frowned back at him. He knew better than to go out without body armor. That Ryder thought he had to *tell* him to wear it pissed him off. But then, Ryder had always been a bossy fuck. Growing up, he'd thought because he was older, he was the king of the fucking hill.

Difference was, this time he *was* the boss.

Just to be contrary, Drake didn't put it on. He stuffed a few more things into his kit and fiddled with his weapon.

It was fun watching Ryder bristle. He stood and flexed his muscles, a snarl on his lips. "Goddamn it, Drake—"

He cut off when Mason clapped him on the shoulder. "He knows," he said. "He'll wear it."

Mason was the only one on Ryder's whole squad who had welcomed Drake in...but then, he and Mason had gone through BUD/S together. They'd been friends for years. He shot him a grateful nod.

It was going to be hell getting these guys to accept him. Ryder especially. Ryder was the most stubborn man on the planet.

"He better fucking wear it." Ryder fitted his belt around his waist and yanked on the end to tighten it. "We don't have room for hotshots on this team."

"I'm not a hotshot," Drake responded. He had to. He just couldn't hold his tongue.

"Really?" Ryder looked him up and down and snorted. "Going in like a fucking cowboy in Kabul?"

"There wasn't time—"

"Do you have any idea what your mom would say if she knew the details of that mission?"

"It's classified." Drake grinned. Okay, it was a smarmy grin, but sometimes Ryder was such an ass.

Ryder's eyes narrowed. "Just keep yourself safe, damn it all anyway. Stay in the back—"

"I am not fucking staying in the back—"

"Listen, you little peckerwood. You asked to be on this team. *My* team. And as long as you're on my squad, you will obey my orders. Do you understand?"

Shit.

He hated it when Ryder went all Neanderthal. He hated it even more when he was right.

As long as he was on this team, Ryder was calling the shots and Drake would obey orders. Even if it killed him.

But it probably wouldn't.

Not if he stayed in the back.

CHAPTER TWO

There was nothing Drake loved more than a night drop. It was a fucking thrill, jumping out of a plane, into the abyss, whistling through the sky like an arrow and then, once the chute opened, gliding silently to the ground.

The team landed on the beach, sloughed off their chute harnesses and switched from jump to assault gear. They skulked toward the target, keeping low and scanning the shoreline. Chatter crackled in Drake's bone phone, keeping him apprised of the team's locations and observations.

When they reached the village they were tasked with clearing, Garrett scanned it for thermal signatures and marked the locations of warm bodies in the sand. It looked like there was one person in each of the four huts and three guards sitting around the fire. Because all the hostages were reported to be in the village at the other end of the island, these were most likely all hostiles, but they'd been cautioned to expect anything.

Ryder assigned Zack, Mason and Tate to take out the guards while Garrett, Luke, Drake and Mr. Fancypants cleared the huts.

Easy-peasy.

With seven targets and seven SEALs, this would be a cakewalk.

They fanned out and settled into position. Zack and Mason quickly immobilized the guards by the fire, and Drake slipped into his target hut.

It was dark, but he had his night-vision goggles on and could see a lump over by the far wall. The lump didn't move, so Drake edged closer. Knowing this could be a hostile, he angled his weapon forward and nudged the bundle.

A snort...and then a snore.

Whoever it was, they slept deeply.

He nudged again. Harder. When that didn't work, he bent and yanked off the blanket and...

Fuck.

He blinked his eyes. Then rubbed them and stared again.

Holy shit.

This was not a pirate.

This was a woman. A woman who could be a Victoria's Secret model. At least, judging from the boobs cupped in a tight t-shirt. Double Ds if he was any judge. And he was. Aside from that, she had a nipped waist and magnificent hips. She lay on her back with her arm over her eyes, so he couldn't tell if she had a face to match that angel's body. For a sliver of a moment, it occurred to him it might not matter.

Even here, in the middle of a mission, she made his mouth water.

Wow.

Just, *wow.*

He knew he was staring, but he couldn't help it.

"I have a target." Ryder's voice crackled over the coms. "Repeat. I have a target."

"Roger that," Drake replied into his mic. "I have a target too."

Garrett and Luke gave the same response.

In a heartbeat, their mission shifted from support to rescue.

The woman stilled and he knew she was awake. She lifted her arm and peered at him through the shadows and then, to his surprise, she reared up and tackled him.

It was a damn good thing he didn't have his finger on the trigger when she did, or he might have shot her. But she did catch him by surprise, otherwise she would never have gotten the best of him, would never have knocked him to the ground and started whaling on him the way Ryder used to when they were kids.

"I told you to leave...me...alone." She punctuated each word with a slam into his chest.

Somewhere in her barrage, she must have realized he wasn't a pirate. Probably when her punches landed on stone-hard ballistic plates. She stopped and stared down at him.

The light from the fire, angling through the door, lit her face and—hell.

Yeah. She was fucking gorgeous too. Perfect. Simply perfect. And she was sitting right on his cock.

Also perfect.

Also hard.

She blinked and frowned at him. "Who are you?"

He sent her a mocking salute. "Navy SEALs, ma'am. We're here to rescue you."

Her perusal of him was not good for his ego. She made a face as she raked him with a sharp gaze. "Really?"

"Really. Could you…get off? We're kind of on a time clock here."

"Oh. Right." She rolled off, and Drake hefted to his feet. With fifty pounds of body armor and gear, it took him longer than he would have liked. Not that he was trying to impress her or anything. This was a mission after all.

He had to remind himself of that.

"Okay," he said, shooting her what he hoped was a reassuring smile. "Let's go. Stay behind me."

He walked her out the door and did a check of the clearing. Zack, Mason and Tate were holding their ground by the fire, scanning the area, ready to provide cover for their retreat. From the corner of his eye, he saw Garrett and Luke heading for the beach with their targets. Ryder had his hostage—a petite blonde—but he hadn't moved out yet. It looked like he was waiting.

For what?

Drake frowned when he realized Ryder was waiting for him.

Goddamn it.

He tapped his mic and reported that he was good to go, but there was no response—nothing but an annoying crackle. Thankfully, Ryder glanced in his direction and Drake gave the hand signal that he was ready to roll. At Ryder's nod, Drake guided his hostage around the hut toward the beach. No doubt, Ryder was following suit.

But then all fucking hell broke loose. A couple yells echoed from the tree line and then the chatter of automatic fire peppered the village, shots going wild. Zack, Mason and Tate edged back and returned fire.

Drake pushed his hostage through the scrub, making sure to keep his body between hers and the incoming rounds. A snarl of pain screamed through his upper thigh and he stumbled, but he kept going. Another round hit the armor on his back and he lurched forward.

A rain of suppressive fire sounded from Ryder's side of the encampment and Drake was hit with twin trails of relief and worry. Goddamn Ryder for drawing fire. He should have bugged out when he had a chance.

As much as he wanted to stay and help the others repel the attack, he knew his mission was to get this hostage to the LZ, and quickly.

Pity there wasn't much quick about his retreat. The muscles of his right leg were numb. He felt like a zombie, dragging one leg behind him, begging for *braaaains*. Someone else was going to have to escort this angel to safety.

What a fucking shame.

"I'm hit, guys," he said into his bone phone. Static flickered back. "Come back?"

Nothing.

Shit.

Coms were often iffy in a combat situation. He tapped the receiver. Fiddled with the connections. Nothing.

Shit.

The weapons fire in the village heated up and Drake heard someone cry out. This mission was going tits up and fast. They needed to boogie. Though he didn't have eyeballs on any of the other members of his team, he'd memorized the map and he knew exactly where to go. He grabbed the woman by the arm and pushed her ahead of him into the trees, traveling parallel to the beach.

They didn't get far, maybe a mile, before he dropped.

No doubt it was the loss of blood that made his head spin, or the pain, but he couldn't go on.

He thrust his rifle at her. "Keep going. Straight down the beach. You'll see the extraction point where the island cuts inland."

She frowned at him. "I'm not leaving you."

"You have to."

"You've been shot."

He tipped his head to the side. "Really? How'd you figure that out?"

"I'm a nurse. I can help you."

"No you can't. You can keep moving down the beach and fucking get on the chopper. When the other guys come by, they'll get me."

"And what if the pirates come by?"

He forced a grin. "They'll get me too."

"Goddamn it," she grumbled. "I hate soldiers."

"I'm not a soldier." His voice was faint because his mouth wouldn't work right. "I'm a fucking SEAL."

Her fingers played around his waist, awfully close to his cock. It was too bad he was worthless to her at the moment. He could feel the sticky warmth of his blood on his leg and he knew there wasn't much time. If the bullet nicked his femoral artery, he would bleed out in minutes.

"You're a fucking hotshot. God, I can't stand your type."

"My type is awesome." Hardly a pithy comeback, but he was—probably—bleeding out.

"We need to get the bullet out. Do you have a first aid kit?" Damn, she was cute when she nibbled her lip.

"In my pack." He waved somewhere behind him.

"And a Gerber?"

He blinked. "You know what a Gerber is?"

"Do you have one?"

"Of course." Everyone carried a multi-tool.

She flipped him over and fiddled around in his backpack for a moment. He really hated feeling so helpless. He was being ravaged by a woman, for fuck's sake.

He didn't mind the ravaging part, as much as the fact he couldn't really enjoy it because he kept drifting in and out of consciousness. Then there was the pain. That was pretty fucking bad too. Not to mention the humiliation…

It only got worse.

Because then she yanked down his pants.

And his underwear.

How mortifying.

He lay on the loam, with his Skivvies down around his knees, with the most beautiful woman he'd ever seen staring at his bare ass…and there was nothing he could do about it.

The welling blackness was a mercy.

* * *

Brandy stared at the wound. It was too dark to see. At least he'd stopped wriggling. She found a glow stick in his pack and cracked it. It was dangerous to do so, but she needed to get that bullet out—preferably before he woke up.

Thank God it was high on his leg, buried not too deep in the thick, roping muscle. A good place to be shot, all things considered. Given that he was still alive and kicking, the round had missed the artery. She tried not to think about those muscles, or the tight curve of his ass, as she sterilized the Gerber and found the slug. It was slippery with his blood, but she grabbed it and worked it out.

He groaned and when she doused the site with alcohol, he thrashed a bit, but he remained unconscious. She covered the wound and tried to lift his leg to wrap the gauze around it, but damn, he was heavy. She had to flip him over to—

Oh crap.

His cock was enormous. She tried to glance away, but her gaze kept drifting back as she worked. She bent his knee so she could reach.

Focus. Focus.

As a nurse, she'd had male patients. She'd certainly seen a penis before…but damn. What did they feed these boys?

She shot a look at his face, and her brain seized. Her attention stalled. He was covered with war paint and tinged in the green light of the glow stick, but a blind woman could tell this was one hot guy. His features were a mélange of hard angles and soft curves. His cheekbones were high and his forehead broad. His nose was long and slightly crooked—as though it had been broken—and his lips were full. He had sinfully long lashes.

That alone made her want to smack him.

It was just wrong for a man to have lashes like that.

She didn't look at his neck, because she knew it was thick and muscled—and she had a thing for necks.

The last thing she wanted, in the entire world, was to have a thing for a squid. She'd had enough of that shit growing up. Her first time had been with a SEAL—in retrospect, revenge against a father who had left them when she was twelve. The romance had been a disaster. *He* had been a disaster.

Never again, she'd sworn. Never again.

She sucked in a breath and finished up the bandage and tried to yank his pants back up, but his big fat ass was lying on them and she couldn't get them to budge. So she tugged up his tighty-whities—trying not to roll her eyes because he wore tighty-whities—and covered his manhood.

Even though it was flaccid, the silhouette was…impressive.

A cry echoed through the trees and Brandy stilled, struggling to hear. Her heart lurched as she recognized the patois of their captors. *Crap*. They couldn't find this guy. They'd kill him for sure. She tucked the glow stick under the arch of his back and lay down on top of him, covering his body with hers.

It was dark. Maybe they wouldn't be seen.

Still, she held her breath as footsteps pounded past. Her pulse rocketed in her ears. Sweat prickled her brow.

Damn. Maybe she should just take off down the beach and…but no. She could never leave him.

Not just because he was a gorgeous dude with a rather impressive package. He was her patient and she'd taken an oath. If roles were reversed, she was certain he wouldn't leave her here. Hell, a warrior like this would pick her up, toss her over his shoulder and carry her away—he seemed that strong—but he wouldn't leave her.

She owed him at least as much.

That was it. Her professional standards. Nothing more.

However, after the pirates passed, she didn't roll off him. Not right away.

And not because it felt so damn…good. They might come back. They could come back at any minute.

That was the only reason.

It was.

Holy fuck. She was lying on him. Her weight was delicious. Her warmth magnificent. The pressure—

Drake's cock stirred.

Okay. Maybe not a stir so much as a full-on woody, shooting up like a fucking heat-seeking missile.

Her head jerked up. She frowned at him.

He grinned.

She grumbled something to herself and rolled off.

Damn.

"Pull your pants up," she snapped. Man, she was cranky. He thought about asking her if she was on her period, but thought better of it. He usually got smacked when he did that.

"*You* pulled them down," he reminded her.

"You're lying on them. I couldn't get them back up. And be careful. Don't rip off the bandage."

He gaped at her. "You bandaged my wound?"

"Of course I did! Why do you think I took off your pants?"

"Um... To check out my ween?"

She did smack him then—on his chest—but it didn't hurt...him. She yelped and shook her hand. At some point she was going to learn that his body armor was hard. "I did not check out your...*ween.*"

"Didn't you?" He was only kidding, but as he sat up, a green glow flooded the space and he saw her blush rise. Hah! She had checked out his ween. But she'd also bandaged his wound, so he decided not to tease her. Too much. "So... What did you think?"

"*What?*"

"Of my wound?"

"It was a gunshot." She glared at him. "I took out the bullet and cleaned it. Wrapped it up."

Wow. All that? How long had he been out? He shifted and a sharp pain lanced him. In the ass. "Am I going to die, Doc?"

She blew out a breath. "Someday...but not today. Now, pull up your pants."

Gingerly, he lifted one cheek and then the other. Another pang. "Shit!"

"Hush," she hissed.

"Sorry." He worked up his pants and fastened them. "Didn't think a tough broad like you would get all huffy over an itty-bitty curse word. You're worse than my mom."

"I could give a rat's ass if you cuss. Just try to keep it quiet. There are pirates crawling all over these woods."

He shot her a glance. "All over these woods?"

"A bunch ran by just before you woke up."

"They did?"

"Why did you think I was lying on you?"

"Um, because you like me?"

She growled. Yeah. Growled. "They would have seen you."

"They would have seen me? So you laid on top of me? Did that make me invisible?"

"Holy God. You're annoying." A muscle worked in her cheek. As though she were gritting her teeth. Or something. "Your skin is lily white. Might as well have a neon sign flashing 'Shoot this guy.'"

Damn it all, she was right. She'd saved his life and he was giving her shit. He swallowed his remorse—it was an easy swallow, because he liked needling her. "Well, thanks." He waved his hand in the vague vicinity of his wound. "You probably saved my ass and I apprecia—"

"No probably about it, Roger Ramjet."

"That's kind of an air force slur."

"I. Don't. Care. I did save your ass." She snorted something that sounded like a laugh…and not a very nice one.

"What's so funny?"

"I saved your ass. Get it? They shot you in the ass."

"They shot me in the leg."

"Looked like the ass to me."

"It was the leg."

She smiled sweetly. "I'm a nurse. I can tell the difference."

He frowned at her. "Well, whatever. Thank you. Now, we'd better get going or we'll miss the chopper. How long was I out?"

"About ten minutes."

"Good. There's still time to…"

Fuck. The dull thud of chopper blades echoed off the marine layer. Drake stared out at the clouds and saw the dark shadow approaching. He knew they'd gone less than half the distance to the LZ. They could try to sprint, but with his leg, they'd never make it.

Crap.

To make matters worse, the pirates she'd warned him about saw the chopper and ran onto the beach yelling and shooting at the sky.

Idiots.

At least they were so focused on shooting at a bird that was out of range, they didn't notice the light from the glow stick. He quickly covered it and they were once again wrapped in darkness.

"Well," she gusted as the cries and retorts wafted into the distance. "What now, Mr. Wizard?"

Drake didn't respond. He was too annoyed with himself to

answer.

Because he'd fucked his end of the mission up.

His first chance to prove himself to his team, and he'd blown it.

And he'd been shot in the ass.

The guys would never let him live this down.

CHAPTER THREE

They had to find shelter. Get some sleep. Her patient needed it, if not herself. And it was pretty clear he couldn't travel very far. At least, not right now. Brandy picked up the glow stick and pushed to her feet.

The SEAL's eyes widened. "Where do you think you're going?"

"I'll be right back. I'm going to scout around for a safer place."

He gaped at her. "Are you fucking kidding me?"

Really? Did he need to squeak like that? "What's the matter? Are you one of those asswipes who think girls can't do anything?"

His lips worked. "I'm not an asswipe."

She arched a dubious brow.

"I'm supposed to be rescuing you. Not the other way around."

"You can barely walk." Ah shit. She shouldn't have said anything…because now he tried to struggle to his feet. She pushed him back down. Again, she shouldn't have, because he landed on a tender spot and yowled. *Yowled.* "Be. Quiet," she hissed. "I'll be right back. I'm not going far." She took off before he could complain some more, moving swiftly, stealthily, scoping out the surrounding area.

Most of the island was little more than scrub and rocks, though there were trees blanketing the coastline. Trees were nice, but they needed more cover than that. She found what she was looking for about a quarter mile down the beach and slightly inland. An escarpment of rocks with a small cave beneath it where the rainwater had washed away the sand. With a couple of bushes obscuring the entrance, they would not be seen from the beach.

It wasn't perfect, but it was a heck of a lot better than being out in the open...or lying on top of him.

Shivers rippled over her skin at the memory of his hardness, his warmth and, yes, the image of his cock. She wished she'd never seen it, but some things could not be unseen.

As she made her way back to him, she found her thoughts returning to that vision, over and over. Which was ridiculous.

Oh sure, he was a mega-hottie. Everything about him was attractive, from the shape of his fuzz-covered head to the alluring V of his hips...pointing straight toward his thick, long—

Shit.

He was hurt. He was her patient. And until they were rescued, they were stuck with each other.

Aside from that, he was kind of a jerk. A brash, bold buckaroo. A navy guy. Just like Charlie.

Charlie, who had wooed her and seduced her and taken her innocence. Oh, her virginity for sure, but a greater innocence as well. Because Charlie hadn't been interested in her. Not really. Charlie had been interested in her father. In advancing his own career.

He'd figured having a relationship with the commander's daughter would benefit him.

Ass.

Yeah, her dad had been a highly ranked naval commander, but Brandy hadn't even *spoken* to him since she was twelve. Since the divorce. Since he'd left them.

She'd discovered Charlie's perfidy by accident, overheard his smug conversation with a friend. His betrayal had devastated her young heart. She reminded herself wounds like that only make you stronger, tougher. Aside from that, it had opened her eyes to the true nature of men. Military men at the very least.

Now she had a thick skin. Now she wore armor. Now she knew better.

She'd had boyfriends. She'd had lots of them. They just didn't wear uniforms.

When she returned to their hiding place she gave a warning whistle, which was smart of her, because the SEAL was on his belly pointing his weapon into the woods. Every muscle vibrated as though he was on high alert. If she hadn't signaled to him, he might have shot her. His head whipped around when he heard her. His wide eyes were like white beacons in the darkness of his camo-smeared face.

He said nothing but waved her down. She hid the glow stick and fell to her knees, holding her breath as yet another patrol passed by. It was pretty clear their current position was along a path the pirates used to go between camps, and as such was unsafe.

When the woods were silent again she turned to her erstwhile rescuer. "I found a spot where we can hide," she whispered. "We should go now, before more of them come by."

He nodded. "How far?"

"Quarter mile. Can you make it?"

His chin firmed. "I have to."

"We'll go slowly." But they didn't. She helped him to his feet and headed out. He moved quicker than she'd expected he could, but he winced with nearly every step. She knew, when they reached their shelter, she was going to have to recheck his wound for bleeding.

They skirted the tree line as they made their way down the beach. He only stumbled a few times, and each time she caught him, but damn, he was heavy. Once they had to crouch in the brush as more calls from the pirates echoed in the night. It was as though the SEAL incursion had stirred up a hornet's nest. Pirates were everywhere.

It seemed to take forever to make it to the outcropping, but it was probably only twenty minutes or so. Time took on a new dimension when your heart was racing.

Brandy guided him into the cave and helped him settle. "Do you have a knife?" she asked. "I want to cut some bushes to cover the entrance."

"Good idea," he said, but it was grudging praise. He fished out a blade and handed it to her.

"I'll be right back."

He frowned. "Be careful."

She responded with a mocking salute. "Aye, aye, captain."

It amused her that his frown darkened.

She'd never been much of a needler, but she sure enjoyed needling him. She wasn't sure why.

It only took a minute to find several full bushes and cut them at the roots. As she dragged them back to their cave, she swept the sand with a serpentine wash to cover any footprints she might have made.

Then she tucked into the hollow and dragged the bushes in behind her, arranging them in what she hoped was a natural-looking configuration.

It wasn't until she settled at his side that she realized how tight the space was with both of them in it, and his gear piled on one side; he'd taken off his pack and his helmet and his communications gear. Hardly any room to move at all. This shelter would work for a while, but it wasn't a long-term solution. She wondered what might happen tomorrow but cut the thought off. She could worry about tomorrow, tomorrow.

"You okay?" she asked as he shifted and grimaced.

"Yeah."

"I should check your wound."

His lip curled.

"It could be bleeding again. Roll over and pull down your pants."

"Seriously? You wanna see my ass again? Twice in one night? Really, honey. I'm flattered."

"Don't be an ass. And my name isn't *honey*."

Despite his snark, he rolled over and, after much fumbling, jerked down his pants. She cracked a new glow stick—the other had burned out—and peered at his wrappings. As she suspected, they were soaked in blood. The wound was to the side, on the crease of his ass. No doubt it had opened with every step he took. It must hurt like the devil.

He glanced at her over his shoulder. "What is it?"

She blinked. "What is what?"

"Your name? I mean, if you don't want me calling you honey, *honey*."

No. She did not. In a big way. "It's Brandy."

"Ah. I'm Drake."

Drake. Her gut twisted. Perfect name for a hot-rod, ramjet SEAL. She forced herself to ignore the emotions that engendered, and to focus on the task at hand. "Give me your first aid kit, Drake. I need to staunch the bleeding and change the bandage."

He riffled through his pack and handed her the kit. "Be gentle."

She tried to glower at his smarmy tone but found her lips tweaking into a smile when he turned away. "Don't be such a big baby."

She didn't bother unwrapping the gauze, but cut it away with the scissors she found in the kit. The wound was seeping but not bleeding freely, which was a relief. With any luck, if he stayed still tonight, it would close up by tomorrow, at least enough for them to move if they needed to.

"This is going to sting," she said as she dumped alcohol on it. He winced and a fresh gush of blood oozed out. She cleaned it, applied a thick bundle of pads and then grabbed a new coil of gauze. "Okay, lift your leg. I'm going to wrap it."

He glanced at her but did as she asked. It was difficult looping the wrap around his hip and thigh, because she really didn't want to encounter anything…intimate. And it was right there. Somewhere. Somewhere close to her hand.

His stiffness made it clear he was aware of her proximity too. His muscles vibrated with tension.

She moved as quickly as she could and tucked the tail of the wrap to hold it. Then she sat back to review her work. "Perfect," she chirped. "Incidentally, it looks like a diaper."

"Awesome." He yanked up his pants, then he rolled onto his back and looked up at her, a solemn expression on his face. "Was it good for you?"

Why she smiled, she didn't know. She tipped her head to hide it. It wouldn't do to encourage him. He was snarky and arrogant and far too good-looking. He was also funny as hell, if she didn't take his comments at face value. Pity she was a sucker for a barbed sense of humor. "You've lost a lot of blood. We need to get you some water."

"I have my camel pack," he said, waving a tube.

"Good. Drink."

"You first."

"I'm not thirsty." She was, but he was at risk of going into shock if he got dehydrated. What a mess that would be. Besides, she had no idea how much water he had in that bladder, or how long it would need to last.

"I'm not drinking if you don't." Damn, he was cute when he put out a lip.

"What? Why?"

"If you pass out, who will take care of me?" This he said in a little-boy voice, but it reminded her she did have a responsibility to keep herself whole too. In this situation, they were in it together. So she drank.

Well, she pretended to drink, making her throat work, but she only took a sip. Though it tasted rubbery, the water was a balm. He watched her with an eagle eye and when he was satisfied he took a sip too.

"Are you hungry?" he asked and her stomach growled.

"Oh my God. Do you have food?"

He chuckled at her enthusiasm. "Kind of. MREs and energy bars. Not the manna of the gods, but filling." He scrounged through his backpack and emerged with a silver packet and a Spork. "Do you like chicken teriyaki?"

Um. Sure. "My favorite."

Because he should stay still, she sat up and fed them both. It was weird, sharing an implement with someone else. In her normal life, she was something of a germaphobe and wouldn't even share a straw with her mother—which made Mom huffy. But seriously. Germs.

She didn't mind sharing with Drake. She had no idea why. Maybe she was just too hungry to care.

The meal was filling, and it didn't taste too bad for something that had been packaged in a silver pouch God only knew how long ago. After they ate, they drank a bit more and then she settled down at his side. "We should rest."

"We should."

"Tomorrow's going to be tough."

"Yep. If I can walk, we should try to get to the secondary extraction point."

"Where's that?"

"On the next island." He jammed his thumb toward the right.

"How far is it?"

He nibbled his lip. "Couple clicks. Can you swim?"

She snorted. "I was thrown into the ocean as a baby."

"Like a Viking?"

"Kinda."

"Okay. We can head out tomorrow. We should wait 'til dark though."

"If you can walk."

"I can walk just fine."

A smile curled her lips. "That saltwater is going to sting."

"Yeah. Thanks for the reminder."

"Anytime." She settled down next to him and closed her eyes. He should have done the same, but he didn't. She could *feel* his gaze on her face. It was irritating. So she opened her eyes and frowned at him. "What?"

He got that look again, the serious one he flashed just before he dropped some joke or snarky comment on her. She steeled her spine in preparation for a hit. Again he caught her off guard. He did that a lot.

"Thank you," he said. Low and soft. Truly sincere, for once. Just *thank you.*

"You're welcome." Something of a grunt. "You'd probably do the same for me."

"Ya think?" He considered this. "I doubt it."

"Why?"

He winked. "I faint at the sight of blood."

"Really? Good thing your wound is...*behind* you."

"Right?"

"In your *ass.*"

"Leg. Remember? That's the story we're telling everyone. It was in the leg."

She smirked at him. "Good luck with that."

"I'm serious. Jesus God." He threw an arm over his face. "Can you imagine what Ryder would say if I came back with an ass shot?"

"Who's Ryder?"

"My squad leader."

Something in the tenor of the words made her ask, "Why do you say it like that?"

Drake blew out a breath. "We also grew up together. He's like...an older brother. He'll never let me live this down."

"Was he on this mission too?"

"Oh, yeah."

"Did he—did he make it out?"

Drake's features clouded. "No idea." He reached over and grabbed his headset and examined it. "Coms went out. Aw. Fuck." He held up a sheared wire.

"Can you fix it?" If they could communicate with the others, she could find out if Lily was okay. Jesus, she hoped she was. Had to believe she was.

"I can try, but I don't really have the tools. And..." He scrubbed his face. "Not thinking too good." He shifted and winced again.

"Does it hurt a lot?"

"Like hell."

She fumbled in her pocket and pulled out a handful of leaves. She extricated one from the jumble and handed it to him. "Chew on this."

"What's that?"

"Qat. It fell out of the pirate's pocket on the ship and I grabbed it." She smiled. "I'm a scavenger, by the way."

"Klepto is more like it."

"That too. Anyway, they chew this leaf. It's supposed to have a narcotic effect."

He reared back. "I don't do drugs."

"Really? Do you take an aspirin if you have a headache?"

"That's different."

"Not really. If you were in a hospital right now, you'd be flying on morphine, and you know it." She thrust the leaf at him. "Just try it. If nothing else, it might ease the pain."

Gingerly he took the leaf and slipped it between his lips.

She tried not to notice those lips. But...damn. They were beautiful.

He wrinkled his nose. "Tastes like shit."

"Eat shit much?"

"You know what I mean."

"Just shut up and chew." She had no idea if the qat would have any effect on him, but it was all she had to offer. She hoped it would ease his pain, at least enough for them both to get some rest.

As he chewed away, staring up at the ceiling, she studied his profile. Deep within her, curiosity burned. She wanted to know what he looked like without the camo streaking his face. Aside from that, it wasn't a bad idea for them both to clean up a bit.

Germs and all.

"Do you have any cleaning wipes?"

"Umm hmm." He found some packets in the pocket of his pack. She ripped one open and scoured her face and hands, then offered him another. She liked that he took it without comment—snarky or otherwise. She liked that he washed his face too. She really liked what he revealed.

But damn. He should have left it on.

Without the goo smeared on his forehead and cheeks, his visage was startling.

In fact, he had the face of an angel—a warrior angel.

She was in dire peril of staring at him all night.

CHAPTER FOUR

Drake settled back and tossed the dirty wipe into a trash bag he'd set up in the corner. Damn, but he liked it, the expression on her face as she gazed at him all googly-eyed. He wasn't sure, but it seemed as though she was drooling. He'd been aware of his good looks since high school—though Ryder insisted frequently he was a troll—but he'd never been more pleased to be blessed in the dimple department than now.

Because if he'd ever met a woman he wanted to impress, it was her. He'd been attracted since first glance, and watching her, seeing how quick and competent and no-nonsense she was, made him like her even more.

She was prickly, to be sure—more so than most women—but he found he liked the challenge. It was hardly any fun if they just fell at his feet. Which they often did. Easy women had never interested him for long.

Her gaze raked over his face, then down to his chest. He didn't need to puff it out, but it was practically instinct. When her perusal reached his crotch, it stalled. Her eyes widened a tad. Because yeah, he was hard. His erection was unmistakable.

He expected her flush—he was feeling somewhat warm himself—but he didn't expect her to say, "Well, good night," and roll over on her side and show him her back.

He frowned.

Damn. It wasn't supposed to work out like that. She was supposed to soften and lean toward him. Invite him in for a kiss or something.

Maybe she was a little *too* prickly.

He didn't know why her reticence annoyed him so much. It wasn't like he'd never been shot down before. Not often, but it had happened.

Of course, she wasn't a typical woman. She was different. From the top of her silky head to the tip of her toes. She was tough and smart and could give back as good as she got. A woman like her didn't take shit from anyone.

She was, probably, perfect for him.

Too bad she didn't see it.

The leaves she'd given him were having an effect, dulling the pain in his ass and wrapping him in a dreamy blanket. No doubt they had dulled his survival instincts too, because he decided to make a play for her.

He was goaded on. By his cock. He'd been rock hard since she brushed his balls while wrapping his wound. No doubt she hadn't intended to touch them, but she had. So it was hardly *his* fault.

"Brandy?" This he offered in a small voice.

The result was successful. She rolled back over and looked at him. "What?"

"I'm cold." It was a balmy night. If anything, he was warm. He shivered nonetheless. "Are you cold?"

"No." She reached for him—his heart lurched—but it was only to take his pulse. Her fingers were soft and sweet on his skin. He imagined what it would feel like to have them…elsewhere. "Your pulse is thready. Drink some more water."

"I don't want water. Can't you just move closer?"

"Closer?" Her eyes narrowed and she peered at him in the dimming light of the glow stick.

"Because I'm cold. Feel my hands." He held them out and she touched them gingerly.

"They are a little cold."

"See. I'm cold."

"How's the pain?"

"Better."

"Is the qat helping?"

"I think so, but it still tastes like shit." He realized, all of a sudden, he couldn't lure her closer and kiss her. Not with his breath smelling like a barnyard. He riffled in his pack, hunting for a mint. Ah. Yes.

He held the roll out. "You want one?"

She frowned but she took one. Awesome. He loved peppermint.

Even more awesome? She scooted closer, right next to him, angling her body along his.

Damn, that was nice. A shiver rippled through him.

She sat up, her hand on his chest. "Are you okay?"

"Mmm." This shiver he faked.

Her frown darkened.

Too much?

He tugged her back down. "This is better."

She grunted but settled in, laying her head on his chest. His fingers inadvertently tangled in her hair. He liked the weight of her on him. Liked her scent, something musky and female. He liked that she wrapped her arm around him and stroked him gently, soothing him.

If they weren't in a cave in hostile territory, this would be heaven.

They stayed that way until the glow stick finally flickered out, encasing them in darkness. Drake was aware of her heartbeat against his chest, the huffs of her breath, the feel of her in his arms.

He closed his eyes and tried to sleep, but couldn't. He was too preoccupied with the fantasies dancing in his brain. He should scuttle them, but they were far too pleasant.

"Brandy?" he asked after a while.

"Mmm?"

"Are you asleep?"

She sighed. "No."

"Do you want to talk?"

"We should rest."

"I can't sleep."

"Okay." She shifted a bit and he tightened his hold so she wouldn't shift away, but apparently she'd just been finding a more comfortable position. "What do you want to talk about?"

"I dunno." He searched for a topic. A topic that would keep her engaged. "Why were you on that ship?"

She blew out a breath. "We were on our way to Kenya and then to Ethiopia. On an aid mission. We were supposed to spend three months in a village building a water system."

"Do you do stuff like that a lot?"

She shrugged. "Occasionally. I work for a nonprofit health agency.

They send us to third world countries and we do inoculations and health screenings in villages."

Holy shit. She was a freaking adventurer.

"What made you want to do that?"

"I always knew I would be a nurse. Or something like that. But hospital work seemed so dull and depressing. This is exciting. Sad sometimes, when I can't help, but mostly exciting. And I love to travel."

"I love to travel too. How does your husband feel about you being gone?" Okay, probably a douche move, mentioning the husband, but a guy had to know.

Her muscles tightened, and then relaxed. "I don't have a husband."

"Boyfriend?"

She growled, but he could hear the humor in her tone.

"Jealous dog?"

The growl became a laugh. "Enough about me. How long have you been a SEAL?"

He took that as a *no boyfriend* and *no jealous dog*. "Five years. Not counting school."

"How many missions?"

He shook his head. He'd lost count long ago. "Lots."

"Wife?"

His pulse stalled, then kicked into gear. "No wife. No girlfriend."

"Jealous dog?"

"Not even. Just my sister Chloe and Mom. They live in Seattle."

"Hmm. Seattle's nice."

"When it's not raining."

"On that one Tuesday in August."

They both laughed. It was heartening that she shared a similar sense of humor. He shifted closer. She let him. "Where do you live?"

"San Diego."

"Oh God." He didn't mean to groan. He'd spent a chunk of his life in Coronado. He knew the town well.

"Yeah. I grew up surrounded by SEAL wannabes."

That explained a lot. Her attitude toward him at least. Townies didn't always appreciate the raucous antics on and off base. "We're not all total jerks."

"I know that." He heard the smile in her voice. "Some of you are only partial jerks."

"That's hardly fair."

"Hey, just calling 'em as I see 'em."

"Go on. Dis the guy who risked his ass to rescue you."

"Ass is right."

They both laughed again. It seemed natural then to curl his arm around her neck and ease her closer. To cover her lips with his.

And shitfire and damnation. She tasted sweet. Of peppermint, certainly, but something more, something elementally female, sweet and irresistible. When he deepened the kiss, easing in his tongue, she let him. Then she met his with hers. When she drew him into her mouth and *sucked*, he nearly came out of his skin.

His blood heated and his pulse thrummed. He rolled over so he was on top—because he really liked being on top—and laced this fingers into her hair and deepened the kiss.

Ah. He'd known. Somehow, he'd known she'd be wild once her passion was roused. He'd thought he'd felt sexual tension between them, but he'd been wrong before.

He was glad he wasn't wrong now.

Her body was a perfect fit with his, soft where he was hard, curved where he was angled. He rubbed against her and whorls of pleasure danced through his crotch. When she rubbed back, they rose to nest in his gut. Goddamn, she was hot.

Her hands scudded over his shoulders and chest, her nails raked his back. Her frenzy rose and she took him along with her—but truly, he was already there.

He'd never kissed a woman in a damp cave before. He'd certainly never kissed a woman in the middle of a mission. But something about it—her limbs tangling with his, the ambient sounds of the night and the shush of the waves, the press of her belly against his cock—something enflamed him.

Or maybe it was the qat.

Whatever.

He didn't care. He was breathless, mindless, wrapped in the tight fist of lust.

As he consumed her mouth, he caressed her, dragging his palm over her shoulders, down her arm to her waist. He delighted in the inward curve, and then skated back up…under her t-shirt. Her skin was warm and silky and it rippled to his touch. She let out a sigh.

He shuddered as he found her breast. Heavy and full. Her nipple was hard, pebbled. He thumbed it. She made a noise in the back of her throat and dug her nails in deeper.

Naturally, he interpreted this as *more*. He gave it to her.

He yanked up her shirt and found her nipple with his mouth. Her bra annoyed him, but he worked around it, tugging it down so he could get a hold on a bare crest. Damn, she tasted sweet. As he sucked and laved and nibbled, drawing the nubbin out to more prominence, she writhed beneath him, making small mewling sounds.

God, he could suck on her all day. He wished he could see. It pissed him off that he couldn't see, but if he stopped to find a fucking glow stick, it might ruin the mood.

She was prickly, after all.

As he fed on one creamy breast and then the other, he unzipped her jeans and slid his hand into her panties. He found her crease and a shudder took him as he felt the cream of her arousal. She was wet.

Holy fuck.

He drew a finger along the slit and then pressed in. He knew when he'd found her clit. Knew immediately. She nearly howled. He stifled her cries with his mouth, kissing her again as he explored her center. Her nub was hard. He teased her mercilessly until she panted and wailed—into his mouth.

It was glorious. Fucking glorious.

He shoved his hand deeper, so he could find her entrance. Not a lot of room to maneuver, but he was a SEAL and used to working in tight places. It took some doing, but he eased down—and in.

She stiffened. Her breath caught. Her grip on his arms tightened. "Jesus," she breathed. "God."

Oh yeah.

He thrust deeper with two fingers. She was tight, hot, wet. It was mind-boggling. His eyes crossed at the thought of fitting his dick into her taut channel. She would be a wild ride. An outrageous fuck.

It was a goddamn shame that couldn't happen. Not here. Not now.

He could bring her to pleasure, though. It was only fair that he give her something back. She *had* saved his life.

He wasn't sure where this melancholy came from. He certainly had no idea from where his restraint sprouted. He'd never wanted a woman as much as he wanted Brandy. It was a damn shame he'd have to settle for having her like this.

He increased his pace, working her, teasing her and then giving her what she needed, wanted, craved.

She came around him in a heated wash, her body dissolving into a series of hellish quivers.

Damn. Damn. Damn. What he wouldn't give to be *in* her.

But that wasn't going to happen. He didn't have a condom. If he had one rule in life…that was it.

It didn't help that, after she'd caught her breath, she reached for his cock. He captured her hand in a tight cuff.

"What?" she whispered, caressing him gently despite his hold.

"We…can't."

She stilled. "We…can't?"

He kissed her. "Baby, I'm prepared for a lot of things, but I'm not prepared for this." *Shit.* He'd never imagined he'd need to prepare for *this.*

"Ah."

"Unless you have a condom…?" It was probably idiotic to ask.

"I do." His heart leaped. "In my suitcase, but I have no idea where it is. The pirates took all our stuff."

It was small consolation that she sounded disappointed, but it was consolation. The fact that she would have let him…well, that she would have let him, was fan-fucking-tastic.

As prickly as she was, she was a lusty minx.

He lurched as she brushed against him again. "Brandy…"

"It's hardly fair that I got release and you didn't," she said in a very serious voice. "What kind of nurse would I be if I left my patient…in pain?" His pulse thudded. His breath caught. His muscles clenched as she undid his pants.

She wanted to play doctor?

Who was he to complain?

CHAPTER FIVE

Unbelievable.

Brandy had come before, but never in a firestorm like that. Her body still trembled with reaction, but the burn in her belly—for more—urged her on. She wanted, ached, for a taste of him.

The vision of his cock had never left her mind. Not really. It had hovered there, an irritation, along with the searing yearning for what she was just about to do.

She loved that he was compliant, silent, tense, as she unzipped his pants and pulled down his briefs—for the third time tonight.

Apparently the third time *was* the charm.

His cock was no longer quiescent, as it had been when she'd seen it before. It was hard and pulsing and, damn, much longer. She swallowed the drool in her mouth and fisted him, aiming his rod for heaven. She swirled her tongue over the fat mushroom head and he hissed in a breath. He tasted salty and sweet, as though a pearl of cum had been waiting for her. She moaned as she took him in, loving his scent—earthy and musky and manly.

His cock filled her mouth. She took him deeper, reveling in the shivers running through his body, the tightening hold of his fingers on her head. He tried to guide her, but she needed no guidance. Wanted none.

She wanted nothing but to ravage him and make him helpless. Make him squirm beneath her. Make him lose all control.

The realization that she had total power over this strong, indomitable man sent a shot of exhilaration through her. She knew whatever this was, it was a one-night thing. It wasn't a relationship or anything like it. They would pleasure each other, relieve the tension, and then, when this was over, they would part.

A trickle of regret sifted through her at the thought but she ignored it. She resolved to focus on the now. On the feel of him as he filled her mouth, her throat. The warmth of him as he shifted and groaned. The power of him as he surged.

She wrapped her fist around his root and stroked, sucking him in a rhythmic motion.

"Shit." His grip on her tightened. "Shit, shit, shit."

She knew he was close. She could feel it in the tautening of his muscles, the ripples of his skin. He sucked in a breath and held it. His intensity swelled.

His cock swelled too.

She cupped his balls, rolling them gently, and he exploded, filling her with jet after jet of his sweet cum. She swallowed it down and lapped for more, cleaning him and soothing him as he caught his breath.

She smiled.

Damn, but that had been fun.

It was too bad when this was all over they'd never see each other again...and it was a damn shame one of them hadn't thought to bring a condom to a rescue.

Because she really would have liked to ride him.

After he came—rather magnificently—Drake was racked with a wave of exhaustion, but it was a pleasant feeling. Part of that could have been the effects of the qat, or the effects of that orgasm, or the effects of his wound. Still he fought it off. He lay there in that musty cave and held Brandy close, enjoying the warmth of her body against his. He didn't want to fall asleep—he just wanted to enjoy this—but, apparently, at some point, he did.

And fuck, he wished he hadn't drifted off, because when he woke up, he was alone.

Anemic threads of sunlight lit the cave; it seemed cold and empty because she wasn't fucking there.

He really loved that Brandy was an adventurous soul and all, but it was damned annoying when a woman got some wild hair up her ass and slipped out of a perfectly safe hiding place to go…to go do whatever it was she'd gone and done.

Panic snarled through him as he realized he had no idea where she was. Or if she was safe. If there were pirates crawling all over this island, why the hell would she slip out to fucking frolic with them?

Drake wasn't used to panic. He wasn't used to not having everything under control. He sure as shit wasn't used to being fucking *helpless*. Frustration and worry bubbled in his gut in a toxic slurry.

Which was probably why he snapped, *"Where the fuck were you?"* at her when she returned with a backpack slung over her shoulder—not even waiting until she was all the way back in the shelter.

She glared at him and finished settling the bushes back in place. They were leafy and full, but it was still possible to see through the lacy curtain to the beach. "Hush."

"Don't tell me to hush! I woke up and you were gone! Damn it, Brandy! I nearly had a heart attack."

"Oh, take a chill pill."

"We're supposed to stay together. You're not supposed to go out on your own."

"You were sleeping."

"You should have woken me."

"Trust me. I tried. Besides, I had to…use the facilities."

"You were gone way too long for that."

"Well…" She tipped her head to the side. "While I was out there, I decided to do some scouting around."

His heart thudded. It was already thudding but this thud was louder…and painful. "Scouting a— What the fuck?"

"For one thing, I wanted to see if I could find any of the others."

"What?"

"I'd like to know my friends are safe."

"Are you insane?" *Was she insane?* There were *pirates* out there. "Of course they're *safe*. Your friends are in the hands of some of the best fucking SEALs on the planet."

There was no call for her to look him up and down in a way that made the hairs on his nape prickle. As though he weren't one of *them*. As though he hadn't kept her safe. He damn well had. He damn well would. If she could keep her ass in the cave, that was.

"Besides, you should be pleased that I did." She shifted the backpack onto her lap with a grunt.

"Where did you get that?"

"I found the spot where the pirates dumped all our stuff. Suitcases and water..." She pulled out a bottle and handed it to him.

He cracked it open but made sure his glower didn't let up. She should *not* have gone out alone. Not. Not. Not. And without a weapon? His blood went cold.

"What if there had been pirates out there?"

"Oh, there were."

Water spewed.

He was going to throttle her. Simply throttle her. His fingers closed on the bottle and a spurt cascaded over his hand. "What?" A croak.

"Yeah. About three. But they were sleeping. So I snuck in and loaded up."

"Are you insane?" The question bore repeating.

She grinned, proving to him, at least, that she undoubtedly was.

"You could have been captured again. Or worse, killed."

Her sigh was heavy. "They're just boys, Drake. They're probably more afraid of me than I am of them."

"Their fear does not make you safe. Men who are frightened do desperate things. *Boys* who are frightened do them with far less thought."

"Oh, quit your belly achin'. I got food too. Real food. Not that MRE shit." His mouth watered as she displayed a can of peaches with Vanna-like panache. He loved peaches. "Do you have a can opener?"

He found it in an eager rush and handed it to her. She seemed familiar with the intricacies of the P-38—which was a miracle—and in short shrift, she opened the can and handed it to him.

As much as he wanted to grab it and snarf it down, he didn't. "You first." That was a rule he'd learned by the time he was five. Ladies first.

Brandy frowned and thrust the can at him again. "Just take a sip. The juice is good. And you need the carbs."

"You need the carbs too. You just went fucking foraging."

She grinned. "I already ate."

"You already ate?" *Without him?* He put out a lip.

"There were some protein bars." She shifted up and a bunch of bars spilled from her pocket. He grabbed one and ripped it open. Manna.

"What else did you get?"

She started unloading items from the bag and he slurped a peach into his mouth, barely restraining his moan of ecstasy. "Clean socks." She sniffed them. "I think they're clean. A fresh shirt for each of us. More food." Cans of tuna, vegetables and fruit. "A bunch of water bottles and…"

He looked at her as she trailed off. "What?"

A flush rose on her cheeks. "Nothing."

Oh, no. Whatever it was, it wasn't nothing. He grabbed the bag and shuffled through the mélange as she tried to grab it back. The glint of a foil package caught his attention. He dove for it. *Whoa, mama.*

His pulse skittered.

He stared at her.

Her blush blossomed.

"Brandy, Brandy, Brandy." He waggled the string of condoms at her. Not one. A fucking string of them. "You are a naughty girl." He couldn't hold back his grin.

She'd enjoyed their, ahem, *playtime* enough to brave pirates with guns to bring him condoms. It was all he could do not to puff out his chest.

Okay, maybe a little.

She waved her hand at the bag. "I just…it was…" She frowned. "They were *there.*"

He leaned forward and whispered, "I love a woman who plans ahead."

"I'm not saying that anything is going to… I just thought… Goddamn it. They were *there.*"

"I get it. Hey, I ain't complaining." He surveyed the long string. He counted seven of them. "You really must think highly of me, though." He winked. "If I weren't injured…"

"Shut up." She snatched them back and shoved them into the backpack.

"Hey. Be gentle with those. We're gonna need them later."

This made her still. She peeped up at him, her expression hopeful. He shouldn't have smirked, because then she glared at him again and snapped, "No, we won't."

"Oh yes, we will."

"You're *injured*."

"Trust me. I'm fully functional. And…" He had to add this. "Last night was amazing."

She grunted.

"Wasn't it?"

"I suppose."

"You suppose?" He edged closer. When she didn't look up, when she kept pretending to riffle the contents of the bag, he lifted her chin. "Tell me it wasn't magnificent." To encourage her to the correct response, he nuzzled her lips. Damn, they were soft and sweet. And yes, she kissed him back. Oh sure, only tentatively at first, but then she really got into it.

He was about to lay her down and test out one of those condoms—or two—when she pulled away and said, "Not now."

He gaped at her. "Not now?"

"No."

"You got something else to do?"

If Brandy could do one thing well and with consistency, it was frown. "Quit being such a horndog."

"I'm not the one who brought all the condoms to the party. You got my hopes up, baby."

"There are pirates out there."

"Sorry, I only like women."

She smacked his shoulder, but he saw her grin. Before she hid it. "That's not what I'm saying. We need to be quiet and you…"

"What?"

She sighed. "You're kind of a howler."

"I am not a howler!"

"Ya kinda are."

He glowered at her. She stared back, her eyes all bugged out, as though underscoring her declaration.

After a moment, he mumbled, "Am not," to which she responded with a snort.

"Let's just eat and rest. We're leaving for the other island when it gets dark, right?"

"Right." He flexed his leg. The wound still ached, but he'd had worse.

Concern flickered over her features. "Will you be able to walk?"

"Sure."

Of course he could.

And if he couldn't, he would anyway.

They spent the day eating and drinking and resting…and talking. Oddly enough, Brandy found she really enjoyed talking to Drake. He was a squid, so it was a new experience for her, enjoying a conversation with one. This was a species she usually avoided like the plague. He told stories of his adventures—the bits that weren't classified—and some of his tales had her laughing her ass off.

She especially enjoyed the recounting of the time he'd gotten drunk on his first unsupervised liberty and had to be hauled out of jail by his commanding officer—and he'd barfed all over his CO's boots.

She knew, from living with her father as a child, that military men were obsessed with their footwear. How many times had she gone into her parents' bedroom to see her father on the bed spit-shining his boots? The smell of boot black and brass cleaner was always a heady scent in the air.

Drake spoke of his sister as well, and the crazy antics they got up to—how they drove their mother crazy. Ryder featured in many of those stories because when they were young, their fathers had been stationed together and their families were longtime friends. It was clear Drake admired Ryder tremendously, that he was the older brother Drake had never had—but when he spoke of him, Brandy didn't miss the downturn of his lips.

She wanted to probe but knew she needed to be subtle.

"So how did you and Ryder end up on the same squad?" It seemed an unlikely coincidence…and a convenient entrée to the real question.

Drake sighed and scrubbed his face. "I asked to be assigned to him."

"Did you?"

"It was my dream to work with him. Always had been. Stupid, huh?"

God, she hated the wobble in his tone. "Why stupid?"

"I don't know. I don't know what I was thinking. That he'd be just as excited to work with me, I guess."

Annoyance rippled in her gut. "He isn't?" She wasn't sure why she was offended on his behalf. Or maybe she was. How dare Ryder disrespect Drake? If she ever met him, she'd rip him a new one.

Drake lifted a shoulder. "He wasn't thrilled. And damn, after this clusterfuck, he'll never trust me again. It was our first mission together."

The hairs on her nape rose. "You didn't do anything wrong."

His chin firmed. "That doesn't matter. I'm responsible. It just sucks to constantly seek the approval of someone who…"

He trailed off, but he didn't need to finish. She knew the feeling and she knew it well. Some people just could not be pleased. Her father was one of them.

"You don't have to prove anything to anyone." She didn't intend to infuse her declaration with such ferocity, but she meant it. "I'm sure your mom and dad are proud of you."

His expression closed down. "My dad, ah, died."

"I'm sorry."

He dismissed her sympathy with a shake of his head. "It was a long time ago. He was a SEAL too and his dad was a frogman in World War II."

"Ah. So you're carrying on the family tradition?"

"I guess."

"Did you ever think of being something else?"

He forced a grin. "Of course. When I was six, I decided I wanted to be an astronaut."

"Wrong branch of the service."

"Don't I know it. But I didn't have the grades to make it in the air force."

"Seriously?"

He shrugged and shot her a grin. Dimples blossomed on his cheek. "What can I say? I was a slacker."

"But not stupid."

"Not stupid. Just lazy. I didn't kick it into gear until it meant something. And by God, when I joined the SEALs, I was determined to make my mark." She knew, she could see it in his eyes…he wanted to make his mark to impress Ryder.

"How'd you do?"

His lips tweaked. "My company all got perfect scores in boot camp."

She lifted a brow. "Hall of Fame company?" Kinda rare.

"Yup."

"Your mom must have been proud about that." And Ryder? Hell, he should be kissing Drake's boots.

He grunted. "She didn't want me to be in the navy."

"What did she want you to do?"

Drake shrugged. "Who knows? Something safe. But you know what? I have a buddy who was killed on the freeway, five miles from his parents' house. Nothing is ever completely safe."

"No." That was certainly true. Brandy had never worried much about being safe. She took life as it came and grabbed it by the horns—if it had any. Life was meant to be lived. It was far too short to have any regrets. There were too many adventures to be had to play it safe.

She glanced over at Drake…just as he glanced at her with *that* look in his eye. This time when he smiled at her, she smiled back.

Life was too short not to taste it all.

CHAPTER SIX

Holy God. Her smile was unmistakable. An invitation, pure and simple. Drake leaned in and kissed her. He'd been thinking about kissing her all day. It was just as sweet as he expected it to be.

There was something about her. About this woman. Something that just grabbed him by the gut and yanked. She was drop-dead gorgeous and built...but it was more than that. He loved her sense of humor and her pluck. He even liked it when she got all prickly, because it was so much damn fun to charm her out of a bad mood.

Each time he made her smile was a triumph, but this smile was probably the best because he knew what it meant. He knew what she wanted.

He threaded his fingers through her silky hair and held her still as he rubbed his lips over hers, then sealed their mouths. She opened for him—he knew she would—and he pressed in.

Fucking heaven.

The intensity of the kiss raged quickly out of control. She clutched at him and he at her and then madly, crazily, she began tugging at his shirt. It was only polite to do the same.

He was thankful it was still afternoon, that some light still shone through the bushes. Because he could *see* her.

Yeah. Much better this way. Her expressions were startling in their feral passion. He liked seeing her skin, the way his dark hand contrasted with her creamy hue. He worked off her bra and took her breasts in his hands. A shiver ran through him. God, he loved her breasts. Alabaster tipped with rose.

He bent his head and sucked her in. As she had last night, she responded with fury, raw passion, arching her back and pressing closer. As he lipped one nipple, he toyed with the other, making her thrash.

He laid her back and ate his way down her body; all the while her hands roved over his bare shoulders, his arms, his back. When she raked him with her nails, he almost lost control. She was like a tigress. A lust-crazed creature of the wild.

Then again, so was he.

He undid her zipper and yanked down her jeans, and her panties with them, baring her.

His breath caught.

She was beautiful. Gorgeous. And yeah, he wanted to gorge. On her. He stroked her mound, traced her, watched as she quivered. Then he opened her with his thumbs.

He glanced up and shot her a somber look. "No yowling," he said, and he bent his head.

She didn't yowl as he lapped her, at least not much, but by that point, Drake didn't care. She kicked off her jeans and wrapped her legs around his neck and held on for dear life as he licked and teased and tormented her clit.

He brought her to the brink of orgasm, working her with his tongue, his lips, his fingers. It surprised him, how quickly she rose into it. But then, maybe not. She was a passionate woman. He loved that her passion matched and met his.

Which was saying a lot because he was hot for her. Crazed. The thought of sinking his cock in her hot folds nearly unmanned him. It certainly befuddled his mind. So much so, he completely forgot about the condom.

She didn't. As he yanked his pants open and tore down his Skivvies, she reached over and fumbled in the bag, cursing until she found them. She ripped one off the string and handed it to him. He tried not to let her see him shake as he opened it and rolled it on, but how could she miss it? She was staring at his cock, her eyes wide, her lips parted.

Damn. Damn those parted lips.

They reminded him of what she'd done to him last night, how she'd sucked and nibbled and brought him to glory.

It took everything in him to wait until she raised her gaze to his.

"Are you ready?"

She gusted a laugh. "Ready? I've been ready for hours."

Yeah. She might just be the perfect woman.

Brandy stared at the top of Drake's head as he fixed his attention on his cock and then, because she didn't want to miss it, she glanced down and watched as he entered her. He'd prepared her well. Her body was open and ready and he slid in easily. One long, slow slide.

Her eyes crossed as he filled her. Gawd, it was good. She shifted her legs apart and urged him deeper. When he winced, she recalled his injury and released her death grip on his ass.

"Maybe I should be on top," she suggested, though without much conviction.

"No fucking way."

"You're injured."

"Shut up," he said, and he kissed her to make sure she did. He thrust his tongue in her mouth as he nudged deeper. The dual sensations sent quivers running through her.

God, he was hot. And hard. And large.

When he pulled out she almost wailed—but remembered they were trying to be quiet. When he reversed direction and filled her again, she couldn't help the whimper that escaped her lips.

It wasn't just the length and breadth of his cock, there was more to it than that. It was a sizzle of electricity when they touched, a flaring excitement that filled her with heat and seething hunger.

"Yes," she huffed, as he came at her from a different angle and kissed a bundle of nerves deep within. Spirals of sensation rocked her. An uncontrollable raft of ripples skittered along every nerve. Damn, he knew what he was doing.

Or, perhaps, they were just a perfect fit.

Fucking had never been this good. Ever.

She came again, almost immediately. She tried to hold it back, but couldn't. He groaned as she closed around him and he didn't move until the quake released her. Then he began thrusting again. This time with a faster, more desperate, rhythm.

She closed her eyes and reveled in the feelings, the bliss cascading through her as he pounded, hell for leather, in and out of her. Like a well-honed spear, he plunged, taking her, time and time again.

Excitement coiled at her core. The beast rose again. She tightened her muscles to fight it off, to make this ecstasy last.

"Relax," he hissed.

"I can't."

"Baby, I can't move."

She frowned at him but tried to relax her muscles. Because really, she wanted him to move. It felt too damn good. And ah. Ah. He launched into motion again.

He stared down at her as he plowed in and out of her, his gaze burning into hers. She loved his face, the way his nostrils flared, the way his chin bunched, the way the muscles on his neck stood out as he strained.

Faster and faster, harder and harder, deeper and deeper still.

His cock swelled, filling her even more, stretching her, consuming her, ravaging her, but she was right there with him. "Yes," she gasped. "More."

"You're killing me, baby," he said on a groan, but he hitched it up a notch.

"You love it."

"God. I do. You're so wet. So hot. Ah!"

He changed angles and hit her again from a different direction and she exploded. Colors danced before her eyes and absolute rapture descended. He lunged once, twice, a third time, and then he shuddered and settled on top of her.

She'd always hated that, when a guy settled on top of her. Felt constricted, locked in. Somehow, with Drake, she loved it. His weight, his heat, the sweat on his brow. She wanted to soak him in. Take it all.

He raised his head and stared at her. His lips worked.

She cupped his cheek and eased up to kiss him. His response was an open-mouthed frenzy. A tumult of lips and tongues and raging gratitude.

"God," he said as he collapsed at her side. "God."

She smiled. It had been pretty fucking amazing. "Imagine what we could do if we weren't in a cave."

He chuckled as he peeled off the condom and dropped it into the trash bag in the corner. "Shit. Imagine what we could do if we had a bed."

"Or a sofa."

"Or the backseat of a Caddy." His grin melted. "But seriously, Brandy?"

"Yeah?" She really liked the look in his eye.

"That was…something."

She nodded. There were no words for it. Just…something. Something beyond belief.

Something that, come tomorrow, might never happen again.

A cold ball formed in her belly. She sat up and found her bra and her shirt and her underwear and her jeans and started putting it all back on.

"Brandy?"

"What?"

"What's wrong?"

"Nothing's wrong. It was fucking awesome. What could be wrong?"

He covered her hand, halting her manic actions. Then he tipped her face up to his and thumbed her tears.

Shit. Was she crying? Why was she crying?

"What is it?"

"Nothing."

"We both know it's not nothing. Did I hurt you?"

"No."

"Then what?"

"Okay. Fine. That was phenomenal. I just had this brain fart, is all."

His brow rumpled. *Fuck.* He was even cute with a rumpled brow. How fair was that? "What kind of brain fart?"

"This thing? Between us?" She swirled her hand in an illustrative manner.

"Yeeeaaah?"

"It's just a one-time thing. The reaction to the situation or some weird chemistry. But when we get back, I'll go home and you'll go back to wherever you hang your hat, and that will be it."

He stared at her for a long moment. His throat worked. "It doesn't have to be like that."

Her heart lurched. "Wh-what do you mean?"

"I mean…" He laced his fingers and stared at them. Unlike her, he seemed absolutely at ease with his nakedness.

She was at ease with his nakedness too. He was magnificent to look at. "Drake?"

"We could agree…this isn't it. We could agree to see each other…after this."

"Is that…? Would you…? I mean…"

"Yes. It is. I would." He glanced at her. "If you would."

Her heart started beating again, this time in a crazed tattoo. Her mood swung up and her soul danced on the clouds. Or something like that. "Oh. I would. I would."

He grinned. "Okay."

"You'll probably drive me crazy before long though," she grumbled. He probably would.

"Likewise." He grabbed his shirt and tugged it on, but she caught his expression before it disappeared. It was stunning. He seemed…delighted and humble and happy.

The realization that he felt it too—that the chemistry or connection or whatever it was wasn't one way—was thrilling.

Sure, he was a SEAL—the kind of guy she'd vowed to avoid for all time—but maybe she needed to rethink that conviction and give this guy a chance. Maybe it was unfair to paint all gung-ho guys with the same brush.

Hell, there was no *maybe* about it.

She couldn't even consider the alternative.

They spent the rest of the afternoon resting and eating and occasionally kissing. Drake knew which activity he liked the best.

And damn, the confirmation that Brandy had enjoyed this as much as he had, that she wanted something more *with him*, was awesome.

He'd had a lot of girlfriends, but none had ever engendered these kinds of feelings, so he wasn't quite sure what this all meant—but he was looking forward to finding out.

Once they got out of this mess, of course.

They started out for the other island as dusk settled on the horizon, but before they left, Brandy made him test his legs. Spending all night and all day cooped up in a tiny cave hadn't done him any favors. Everything was creaky and stiff.

His ass hurt with each step and he was weaker than he would have liked, but they made sure to eat plenty and drink up before they left, so he had faith he could work that all off.

He'd been in worse shape. Once, he'd run ten miles with a massive hangover. Next to that, this was a fucking cakewalk.

Brandy led the way down the beach, which he found annoying—he was the one with the weapon after all—but if they were going to try to have a relationship after this, he figured he'd best learn to live with her tendency to forge onward...without his approval. Besides, she'd made this trek before.

She slowed as they approached the clearing mounded with supplies. Drake scanned the area and determined no pirates were around. They stocked up on more water and food and continued to the south. They didn't know how long they'd have to wait on the other island once they got there. Might as well be comfortable.

He wasn't looking forward to swimming in the ocean—not with his wound—but mentally, he was preparing for it. He'd do whatever it took to keep her safe.

Brandy rounded a corner and skidded to a halt. Drake lifted his weapon, even as her hands rose slowly in the air. She shot a remorseful look at him over her shoulder and his gut lurched.

He peered around the tree and froze. His heart thudded painfully. His breath caught.

Shit. Fuck.

A group of pirates stood in the sand, holding AK-47s pointed directly at her.

"Back up," he hissed.

She obeyed—thank God—taking a tiny step back. She flinched as one of the pirates fired; a bullet hit the sand at her feet. "Drake?"

They couldn't see him yet. Maybe he could whip around and open fire and take them out before—

But no. They had their guns up. Their fingers on the trigger. If he shot, they would too, and they would hit her.

"Go on. Get away," she whispered.

He didn't.

He couldn't.

For one thing, he would never leave her to the mercies of a band of pirates, not now. Now that he *knew* her.

And then there was the sharp nudge in his ribs from behind.

They were surrounded.

Yeah. Awesome.

His first mission with Ryder's squad and he'd gone and gotten himself captured by the enemy.

On the upside, wherever they took him, Brandy would be there too.

Well, he was wrong about that.

The pirates marched them both to the south, which was good, because if they managed to break away, they'd be that much closer to the beach where they needed to cross to the other island. They headed straight for the village on the south shore, the one the other squads of his team had raided…was it only last night? Now the village was empty except for the pile of bodies on the sand at the tree line. There were signs of a firefight everywhere. Bullet holes in the trees, a doused blaze on the roof of one of the huts…blood in the sand.

He edged closer to Brandy, but the pirates ripped them apart, urging them to separate huts. Drake's soul wailed. He wanted to be *with* her. She cried out as one of the pirates pushed her and she fell.

He bristled and lunged but couldn't break away from the three pirates holding him. One of the bastards slammed him on the skull with the butt of his rifle and he went down. Bile rose as pain flooded him. His head spun.

"Fadlan. Tur. Dhaawacmay!" Brandy called. At first, Drake thought maybe he had a concussion or a stroke or something, because she was talking gibberish…but then the pirates spoke back to her in the same gibberish.

When she said something like, *"Waxaan ahay kalkaaliye caafimaad,"* they stilled and spoke amongst themselves. Then, glory be, they dragged him into her hut.

That they dropped him on the floor in a pile was small consolation. He groaned as he struggled to his knees.

"Don't." She pushed him back down. "Don't or they'll tie us up."

He scrubbed the back of his neck and winced. "Tie us up?" Okay, he was still a little fuzzy from that hit.

"Just relax. We have food and water." They'd riffled through her backpack but had handed it back. His weapon and pack, however, they'd taken. He'd get them back if it killed him.

You didn't fuck with a SEAL's pack. You just didn't.

"What did you tell them?" he asked.

"I told them you're injured and I'm your nurse."

"Clever girl." He kissed her. "I didn't want to be separated."

"Neither did I." She sighed. "Do you think you're up for an escape attempt?"

He frowned. "I think they'll be watching pretty close. After everything that's happened."

"Probably."

"But they're not too bright..." He grinned at her. He loved the way his smile seemed to calm her.

"Not very. But let's take it one step at a time. Pretend to sleep if they come in and then, in the night, if we can, we'll slip away."

"We're close to the beach. It's just a hop, skip and a jump from here."

She chuckled. "You forgot to mention *swim*."

He grimaced. "No, I didn't. I just don't want to think about the swim."

But it hardly mattered, because shortly thereafter, their captors came in and tied them hand and foot.

Drake glanced at Brandy as the pirate yanked hard on the binding at his wrists. He winced. They were not much gentler with her. The fucks.

Bound and helpless, they lay down side by side. She sent him a sad smile and he offered a brave grin in response.

The situation seemed hopeless. He saw as much in her eyes.

But he was a SEAL. SEALs never gave up.

There was a way out of this. He'd prove it to her if he died trying. And he might.

CHAPTER SEVEN

When the pirates left, closing the thatched door behind them, Brandy blew out a breath. What a dismal circumstance. The only positive was that she and Drake were together.

"Are you okay?" she asked into the darkness. It had been horrible rounding that corner to find herself facing the muzzles of so many guns. Horrible being manhandled and pushed down the beach. Even worse? Seeing Drake get clobbered. Seeing him fall to his knees. He still seemed a bit dingy. She hoped he didn't have a concussion.

"Hmm?"

He was rustling around as though he couldn't get comfortable on the hard dirt.

Yeah, neither could she.

"Are you okay? How's your head?"

"Hurts."

"And your vision? Is it blurry?"

He barked a laugh though there was little humor in it. "Everything's dark, Doc."

"Ha ha. Did it go blurry after they hit you?"

"I saw stars." A grunt. More rustling.

"What are you doing?"

He stilled. "Nothing." The way he said it made Brandy suspect his mother had heard that exact response more than once…when he was up to no good.

"Drake—"

"Ah. Yes." A snap echoed through the room, and then the sound

155

of sawing.

"Drake? What are you—?"

"Hush, Brandy. Give me a minute—"

She shook her head and listened, trying to make out the sounds. She jumped when he sidled up behind her. "What—?"

"Hush, honey."

"How did you get loose?"

"I had a knife in my boot. They aren't very good at frisking people." His breath washed over her cheek as he untied her. She had a sudden urge to kiss him. God, he was amazing. Then realization skittered through her and something cold settled in her belly.

"You're not going out there." She could still hear the pirates moving around.

"No. I'm not going out there…"

The way he trailed off concerned her. "Drake…"

"I'm not going out there…yet."

Shit. "Drake. They have *guns.*"

"I have a knife. I'm trained for combat. I can take them out. What were there? Six of them?"

"Eight."

"Piece of cake."

There was no tremble in his voice, only brash confidence. Surely he was delusional. "I think we should stick to the plan. Wait until it's quiet—"

"Oh, I will."

"And sneak away. It's insane to try to battle them all."

He sat down beside her with a *humph.* "They have my pack. And my weapon."

"Let them have them."

"It's *my* stuff."

"It's better than letting them have your life. Drake, I couldn't bear it. I couldn't bear it if they hurt you or…" She couldn't even say it. She did kiss him then. Hard, hot, rash. A pleading kiss. *Don't leave me.* She wouldn't say the words, but she let her passion speak for her. "We're going to explore this thing, remember?"

"I remember. How could I not remember?"

"I need you whole."

"Brandy, they have my *stuff.*"

"Fuck your stuff. I'll buy you a new backpack—"

"You don't understand. If I return to my squad, shot in the ass and stripped of my gear…"

"What? Ryder might frown at you? Big whoop-de-fuckin-do. By the way, I'm seriously not liking this dude."

"Ryder? Don't say that. He's awesome."

She stroked his cheek. Kissed him again. "He doesn't sound awesome. Not if he can't see what a freaking hero you are."

He stilled. "You think I'm a hero?"

"Of course you are. With a gun, or without it."

A snort. "You don't call it a gun."

"What?"

"It's a weapon." He took her hand and set it on his crotch. Unbelievably, he was hard. "*This* is a gun." He chuckled as though he'd told a joke. A Man Joke. About penises.

She sighed. Only a SEAL could get a woody in a situation like this. "Whatever. Please. Just stay here with me until the camp gets quiet. Then we'll slip away and swim to the other island. Promise?" When he was silent, she gouged him with an elbow. "Promise."

"Oh, all right." Crickets chirped outside their hut. Conversations from the fire rose as the pirates chatted. And then, after a long moment, Drake murmured, "But if there's a chance to grab my stuff…I'm going for it."

What a baby. "Fine."

"Fine."

"Good."

"Good."

She didn't care that his tone was a touch petulant. All she cared about was that he'd promised to stay by her side.

Suddenly, that was what she wanted more than anything in the world.

It took for-fucking-ever for the pirates to settle down. It pissed Drake off that they were celebrating this capture. He wanted to storm out there and punch them all in the face, but he'd promised Brandy he'd wait, here, with her. Once he had a chance to calm down, he realized it was the best plan.

He hated the idea of leaving his equipment behind—he felt naked without his weapon—but if he had to choose between getting her to safety and grapping his crap, the choice was obvious.

Their captors came in a couple times to check on them, and Drake and Brandy kept the rope looped around their ankles so it looked like they were still tied.

Each time it took everything in him not to leap up and accidentally break someone's neck, but he knew more pirates were out there, so he tried to behave.

It sucked.

When several hours had passed and they determined it was quiet enough to check the clearing, Drake crawled to the door and eased it open. There was a fire in the center of the village and it was surrounded by pirates, all of whom looked to be asleep. He couldn't see his pack or his weapon. They'd likely stored them in one of the huts, which meant they were lost to him. He couldn't risk a search.

The moon had decided to come out tonight—*fuck it all anyway*—so a dim light illuminated everything, but their hut was near the edge of the village, so if they moved quickly and stayed low, they could make it to the tree line where they would have cover. He waited a moment or two, to make sure there wasn't a guard patrolling the perimeter, and then motioned to Brandy.

Together, they slipped from the hut and crawled over to the trees. Drake levered up onto his haunches and dog-walked into the woods. Brandy followed. Once they were under cover, they stopped and peered back at the camp. Still quiet. A good sign.

Drake signaled Brandy to follow him, but of course she didn't. He would have sighed, but he was trying to be as quiet as possible. He rose up and followed her, staying hunched down.

His heart thudded in his throat as they moved through the stand of trees. The sand was soft, so their footfalls made no sound. The scent of the ocean brine teased his nostrils. So close. They were so close.

The sight of the moonlit ocean between the boughs sent a scud of excitement through him. All they had to do was slip into the water and swim, and they would be safe.

He halted her before they hit the beach, and he did a quick reconnoiter. Nothing.

Perfect.

Glancing at her, he nodded. "You ready to swim?"

"Ready."

As one, they sprinted for the water.

A cry rose up behind them and he sped up, urging her on.

Shit. Why hadn't he seen the pirate skulking on the brush?

Rapid fire retorted over their heads. Drake ducked down and Brandy followed suit.

More shouts. More calls. More rifle blasts.

A bullet whizzed by him and he ran faster. Almost there. Almost…

A round hit him in the leg and he stumbled, but he didn't stop. It was only a bullet. He wouldn't let it stop him. But fuck. It slowed him down. "Go," he yelled at her.

Her eyes were wide, wild as she glanced back at him.

To his horror, she slowed, wrapping her arm around him and helping him limp toward the water. He tried to break away. "Go. Just go."

"No. We go together." She looked over her shoulder and paled. "They're gaining on us."

"Jesus, Brandy, just fucking go."

"I'm not leaving you."

They hit the surf, splashed into the water. If he could just get deep enough, he could swim—

A hard hand grabbed his arm, and another. And a third. Brandy's cry echoed in his ears as they grabbed her too, and none too gently. One of the pirates tackled her and wrestled her to the ground. From the corner of his eye he saw the fucker land a punch on her cheek. She slumped.

Fury raged.

He whirled, shaking off the pirates holding him, and stormed over to the fucker who dared to touch his woman. No way. No goddamn way would he hit her and live.

He plowed into the pirate, pinning him, pummeling him with one hard slam after another. It was glorious watching the blood spurt from his nose.

The bastard had touched his woman. Hurt her.

He needed to die.

A deafening blow to his head slowed his fists, but he didn't stop pummeling. It was followed by a second and a third.

It was the fourth that did him in.

Pain shot through his brain, bright screaming lights that coiled with the burning agony in his leg. His breath caught. His head spun.

And he fell.

His last thought before the darkness took him?

Not that he'd failed his mission. Not that Ryder would be disappointed in him.

But that he'd failed *her*.

Utterly.

Completely.

Brandy watched in helpless horror as the pirates beat Drake about the head and neck with the butts of their rifles until he fell. He collapsed, face-first into the water, and something cold crawled along her veins.

"Get him out!" she screamed, surging forward, fighting their hold, but they didn't seemed inclined to pull his face out of the water.

He was going to die.

To die.

Right here before her eyes. In three inches of water.

No. No. No!

She turned and racked the man holding her in the groin and, when he wheezed and released her, she ran to Drake and turned his body over.

Even in the moonlight, the curl of blood around his head was chilling. She stared at his chest, praying for a rise, a movement, anything.

Nothing. His face was pale. His beautiful lashes made sooty arcs on his cheeks.

"Drake!" she cried, shaking his shoulder. "Drake. Wake up, damn you."

When one of the pirates grabbed her arm to drag her away, she snarled at him and he leaped back, a look of shock on his face.

Brandy thrust her terror aside and went to work, tipping Drake's chin, pinching his nose and placing her mouth on his. One breath. Two. She checked for a pulse. Oh, thank God. He had one. It was thready, but there.

She breathed for him again. And again. Lifted a lid. Checked his pupil. It wasn't blown. That was a good sign.

How many hits could a man take on his skull before there was permanent damage? She didn't want to know.

She kept breathing for him until he groaned and opened his eyes. They were slightly crossed. Then he focused on her. "Brandy."

Relief gushed through her. "Drake. Baby. Are you okay?"

He smiled. It was the most beautiful smile she'd ever seen. "It's just a scratch," he murmured, and then his eyes closed again.

When she leaned back, the pirates rushed in. Two of them grabbed Drake by the arms and dragged his limp form back onto the beach. One of them tried to grab her but she glowered at him. He backed away. "Be careful," Brandy snapped, following along.

Oh, what a fright. She'd never been so scared. Not even when she saw the pirates roaring toward their ship. Not when they'd gunned Pierre down as he tried to escape.

Nothing had ever hit her this hard, and not because she felt responsible for him, or because they'd come through this adventure together.

But because it was Drake.

She didn't completely understand the feelings swirling in her heart and soul, but she suspected what this unfamiliar emotion was. It seemed inconceivable. Truly it did. They'd only known each other for two days…but it seemed like a lifetime.

And the heart didn't lie.

This had to be love.

Finally. After all her searching.

What a bitter irony that neither of them was likely to come out of this alive.

CHAPTER EIGHT

Apparently, the pirates had learned their lesson. They didn't put their captives into huts. Instead, they built up the fire and kept her and Drake close at hand. They allowed her to tend him, even brought her the first aid kit when she asked for it.

Okay, demanded it.

She cleaned up the mess on the back of his head and was relieved to see it wasn't as bad as she'd feared. Head wounds tended to bleed profusely. She knew this. It was the goose eggs she was worried about. Too much swelling was a bad thing.

Her captors watched with much amusement as she peeled off Drake's pants and, again, dug a bullet out of his thigh. This one, on the other leg, hit the muscle—no wonder he couldn't run. Fortunately, it was far from the artery. She changed the bandage on his other wound because it was soaked with seawater, and she didn't know when she'd get another chance.

Indeed, when she finished, and had dressed him again, they bound her hands, and Drake's too. She resigned herself to the fact that there would be no more escape attempts, at least for the time being, and settled down at his side to sleep.

It was a restless night. The pirates kept talking and every time Drake moaned, she would come to wakefulness and check him. When she wasn't sleeping, or wondering what the morning might bring, she was praying. Praying to God that he survived. She didn't think she could stand the world without him in it.

How freaking ironic. She'd always wanted to find love, to find a man she wanted to be with…forever. And now that she had, forever might be a very short while.

Drake still hadn't roused when morning dawned. He slept through the meager breakfast the pirates provided, and lunch. At one point, early in the day, her heart leaped as she thought she heard the thud of chopper blades. In her delusion, she imagined it was the cavalry on its way to save them. The pirates all jerked up too and hoisted their weapons, but because of the marine layer, she saw nothing and no one came.

Her mood slumped.

Drake needed professional help. He'd taken two bullets and more hits to the head than she could count. There was little she could do to help him, but a doctor with a full sick bay could.

Her annoyance at the navy for forgetting about them grew.

Around late afternoon, Drake stirred. The first word out of his mouth as he turned his head was, *"Fuck."*

"Be still," she said, laying her bound hands on his forehead. "You're hurt."

"Ya think?" His blue eyes opened. Her heart lifted at the sight. They were clear and beautiful. His pupils were even and reactive to light. "I'm aware I've been injured. Shit." He winced again. "Everything hurts."

"They hit you on the head until you passed out. And they shot you again."

He frowned. "In the ass?"

"In the leg."

"Oh, thank God."

"I got the bullet out."

His lips tweaked. "Of course you did."

"But you've lost a lot of blood. Don't move or you'll lose more."

He shrugged. "Where am I gonna go?" Still, he forced himself into a sitting position. The guard watching them lifted his rifle. Brandy glared at him until he lowered it.

She opened a water bottle—no mean feat with her hands tied together—and helped Drake drink. "God, that tastes good."

"Not too much. Just sips." She handed him an energy bar. The pirates had tried them and not liked them, so they'd let her keep them. Drake wolfed one down and she gave him another. There weren't many left, but he needed them more than she did.

When he finished eating, he shot her a dark look, but he didn't say anything.

"What?"

"Nothing." He glanced away, but not before she noticed his expression. Regret. Remorse.

"What is it, Drake?"

"I'm sorry, Brandy. I'm so fucking sorry."

"It's not your fault."

"It kinda is. If I'd been faster—"

"They would have caught us. Or shot us in the water." She'd thought a lot about this last night, and the truth was inevitable. As sucky as it was, being captured was far from the worst thing that could have happened.

"Still. It was my job to—"

Another pirate stomped up to the fire and scowled at their guard, a boy, and then scowled at them. "Shut up. No talk."

Drake ignored him. "I'm sorry, is all. I wish—"

The pirate stormed over and hit Drake in the ribs. He fell to the side with a groan.

Brandy scuttled over him as the pirate lifted his rifle to hit him again. "No!" she cried. "Leave him alone."

The pirate frowned. "Shut up. No talk."

"No talk," she agreed, but then she added, "no hit." She wanted to add more, like, "If you hit him again, I'll kill you, you fucker," but decided it might be more prudent to hold her tongue. Also, the bastard's grasp of English was limited to two-word sentences.

After that incident, they didn't speak again, but Brandy sat next to Drake and surreptitiously rubbed his back so he knew she was with him. So he knew she didn't feel like he'd failed her.

He hadn't failed her. Not in any way.

She only hoped that at some point she could tell him that.

Agony racked him. In his head, his neck, his back, his leg…his ass. He felt completely worked over. On top of everything, he felt weak and shaky and he was in a dismal mood.

He knew Brandy didn't see it, what a complete fuckup he'd been, but he saw it. He knew. His crazy-ass idea to run for the water could have gotten her killed. *Killed*. As it was, it had nearly been the end of him.

It was mortifying to sit next to her, trussed up like a pig. A man wanted to be a hero to his woman. He was far from that.

On top of all that, their future was uncertain. These bastards could decide to just turn their guns on them and be done with this whole debacle. Some of the younger pirates looked like they were ready to do just that.

As the day wore on, his mood got darker and darker. It wouldn't be so bad if he could talk to her, but he couldn't. It got to the point where he couldn't even bear to look at her. So he stared out at the woods. And brooded.

A flicker of movement, a flash of light, caught his eye. He honed in on it. His heart lurched. Was that—?

Fuck, yeah. It was. There in the brush. The unmistakable muzzle of an MK17 long-barreled assault rifle.

He tried not to giggle, but relief and a wash of vindi-fucking-cation rushed through him. A glove appeared, motioned. Drake nodded, but barely.

He yawned. "I'm gonna lie down," he told no one in particular, but he glanced meaningfully at Brandy.

She gaped at him and then got the message. "Yeah. I'm kind of tired too."

He liked that she nestled up behind his back. "Stay close," he whispered.

She knew better than to respond. Or argue. Indeed, her muscles hummed with a sudden tension.

Not a moment later, three squads of heavily armed men dressed in full SEAL kit swarmed into the compound, bellowing and waving their rifles at the knot of pirates. Almost to a man, they dropped their weapons and raised their hands.

Drake had never seen a prettier sight.

It was all he could do not to crow.

With the pirates held at bay, his buddy Mason rushed over to them, his knife ready to cut their bonds. "Are you okay?" he asked.

"Mace, damn it. Never been happier to see your face. We're fine. But Brandy first."

She snorted. "No. Drake first."

Mason rolled his eyes and did what he should have done, slicing through Brandy's bonds like they were butter. Then he commanded her to run to the back of the pack of SEALs.

"But—"

Of course she would argue. "Go, baby. I'm right behind you." And thank God, she did. As Mason got to work on his ropes, Drake watched Brandy run into the circle of big bad motherfuckers. It closed around her.

Yeah. Not a more beautiful sight in the world.

Mason fixed him with an amused gaze. "Did you just call her *baby?*"

"Maybe."

"Shit, Drake, what the hell happened on this island?"

"What do you mean?" His bonds fell free and Mason held out a hand to help him up. Normally, he would never take it, because he was a goddamned SEAL and he didn't need help from anyone, but his legs were wobbly.

Drake slipped his hand into Mason's, but before his buddy could haul him to his feet, a pirate ran out from one of the huts, screaming, gun blazing. Three rounds hit Mason square in the chest.

Thump. Thump. Thump.

It was a sound Drake would never forget. His buddy lurched back and fell flat on his back, his eyes closed.

"Fuck!" Drake's cry was drowned out by the retort of return fire. It only took a second to cut down the pirate, but it was a fucking second too late.

Drake scrambled to Mason's side and ripped open his shirt.

Ah. Thank God. The plates had stopped the bullets. But Mason was still. Too still.

"Mace?" He shook his shoulder. "Mace?"

Fuck! He wasn't breathing. Drake gave him two breaths and then yanked off his vest, ripped up his shirt and stared at his bare torso, watching for a rise. Nothing. *Goddamn it!* A vest could stop a bullet, but impact to the chest could still stop a man's heart. "Medic!" He started doing chest compressions and rescue breathing as the medic dashed over with the AED.

As the medic cut off Mason's shirt, applied the pads and primed the machine, Drake could hear Brandy yelling and Ryder calling out commands, but he didn't dare look up. Mason couldn't die. He was Drake's *friend* for Christ's sake. He was the only man on the squad who even liked him.

Shit.

His compressions became more manic.

One breath. Five compressions.

One breath. Five compressions.

One breath. Five compressions.

What the fuck was that medic doing? "Where are you?" he barked. "Where are you, man?"

"Charging. Give it a sec."

"He doesn't have a sec." One breath. Five compressions. *Oh God. Oh God. Oh God.*

The tone sounded. "Clear."

Drake reared back, holding his hands away. Mace's body lurched as the shock snarled through him. Drake stared at the machine, watching the tiny screen. The atonal whine of the monitor was starting to piss him off.

"Still in V-fib," the medic said. "Charging."

Drake resumed his breaths, but Ryder took over the compressions. After a minute or so, the medic called "Clear" again and ran another shock through Mace's body.

And again.

And again.

Drake's panic rose. He knew Mace's chances were slipping away. When Ryder clapped him on the shoulder and said, "Drake, it's over," he whirled on him.

"It's not over. It's not." He gored the medic with a dark glower. "Charge it again."

"Drake—"

"Charge. It. Again."

The turd glanced at Ryder before he complied, but Ryder must have nodded, because he pressed the button to charge, and Drake continued his breaths. If Ryder hadn't nodded, he would have knocked his fucking head off.

Maybe he knew that.

Or maybe he didn't want to lose Mason either. He was a damn fine man. He deserved better than to die from a coward's fucking ambush.

"Clear."

Drake pulled back. *Please, Mace,* he prayed. Knowing, in all likelihood, this was his buddy's last chance. *Please.*

The shock took the body in slow motion, arching it up in a macabre dance.

It seemed to take forever. The pause between the shock and the machine's response, longer still.

But—*thank you, Jesus*—it wasn't an atonal whine.

This time the machine kicked into a beeping rhythm.

Drake nearly collapsed on the sand. From relief, yes, but from Ryder's clap to his back as well.

"Holy shit. We did it," Ryder said, whipping him into a bear hug.

"We did." Drake nodded to the medic. "Thanks. I...um, sorry if I yelled."

The medic winked. "I'm used to it. Come on in, boys. We need to get this man back to the ship. He needs attention."

The squads swarmed in, Rocco's crew taking charge of the prisoners and Buzz's fanning out to check the other huts and the woods. Ryder's squad came for their man. Drake rose to his feet...and then sank back down. Yeah, his legs wouldn't hold him. It was the shits, but he was probably going to have to be carried out.

"Come on, brother." Ryder grinned and cuffed him on the shoulder, nearly tipping him over.

"Stop that!" A shrill voice cut through the clearing. Ryder froze. He lifted his gaze; it stalled on Brandy as she marched toward them, more intimidating than any admiral.

"Excuse me?" Ryder clipped in his most commandery voice. He had that look on his face, the look that made most men piss their pants.

Brandy faced him, toe-to-toe, and stared him down. Her expression was pretty damned intimidating too. "This man is injured. Stop knocking him around."

"It's okay, Brandy. This is Ryder." Buddies did that. She oughta know. They knocked each other around all the—

"Oh." She crossed her arms and raked Ryder with a scorching assessment. Her lip curled. "So you're *Ryder.*"

Ryder blinked at her vitriol. His brow rippled. "What does *that* mean?"

"The asswipe who doesn't *approve* of him."

Oh. Fuck. She needed a muzzle.

"What do you mean?" Ryder shot a puzzled look at Drake, and then helped him back to his feet, but Brandy stepped between them and wrapped his arm around her neck. As though *she* could carry him.

"You know damn well what I mean, *Ryder.*"

"I approve of him—"

"Hah. You didn't want him on your team—"

"Of course I didn't want him on my team."

Drake flinched as Ryder admitted the truth. He'd known it, but he'd never heard it from his lips.

Brandy snarled. Actually snarled.

Ryder winced. "Damn it. I wanted him somewhere safe. He had his choice of any assignment. He could be on the admiral's butt-wiping detail if he wanted. Rather than out here, risking his life every day—"

"Getting shot…" This, Drake added, because he thought it sounded impressive.

Ryder paled. "So you did get shot?"

"Twice." He glanced meaningfully at Brandy. "In the *leg.*"

"Fuck." Ryder scrubbed his face. "Your mom's gonna kill me."

"Mom doesn't need to know."

"She made me swear to keep you safe."

"I'm fine." He wobbled a bit, but then so did Brandy as she took more of his weight.

Ryder snorted and took his other arm, keeping him from crumbling to his knees. "We need to get you to sick bay and get those bullets out."

"They're out." Damn, her voice was sharp when she was pissed. He wouldn't want to be Ryder right now, on the pointy end of her temper…but it was fun to watch.

"How did, um, how did you get them out?"

Brandy sniffed. "I *took* them out."

"With my Gerber," Drake said with a tinge of pride. Yeah. She was his woman. And she was a badass.

"Oh, Christ."

"She's a nurse."

Ryder studied her for a moment. "Thank you for saving him—"

"He saved me," she retorted. "Again and again." She left his side then so she could whirl around and poke Ryder with a pointy finger. Without her support, Drake listed to the left. Tate stepped in to prop him up. "He's a hero." She punctuated each word with a savage thrust.

Ryder winced. "I know he's a hero! You don't have to tell me he's a fucking hero."

"You could tell *him* that once in a while."

"Goddamn it, Drake, you're a fucking hero!"

"I know." But they both ignored him.

"Well, fine," Brandy clipped.

"Fine!"

"Good."

"Good."

Okay. As entertaining as this was to watch, Drake didn't like her attention on any other man. He didn't like the way they stared at each other. He really didn't like the sizzle of tension between them. He cleared his throat. When Brandy didn't stop glaring at Ryder, he said, "Ow."

Her attention snapped to him. "Oh, baby, are you all right?"

"Baby?"

Drake ignored Ryder and Tate, focusing on Brandy. "I'm fine. But it hurts." He put out a lip.

She shot a frown at the men surrounding him. "What the hell are you waiting for? Let's get this man some help!"

They launched into action then—how could they not, after such an order—leading him through the village and onto the beach. He was determined to stay on his feet, to walk like a man, but every step was agony. It was an enormous relief when the Chinook landed and they piled on and he could sit...though even that stung. Brandy pushed past Ryder to take the seat at his side. She put her arm around him and glowered at the squad. Naturally, they all looked away.

Cowards.

As the chopper took off, Drake's gaze locked with hers. "We're safe," he said, though there was no way she could hear him over the drone of the blade.

"We're safe," she mouthed back. And then she kissed him.

Not a fleeting buss, but a full-fledged *holy-shit-we're-not-gonna-die* kiss. It was magnificent.

She kissed him all the way back to the USS *Sierra Nevada* and kept kissing him as the rest of the squad filed off to head for the debrief. All but Ryder.

He grinned at the two of them when they surfaced; it was a wicked grin. It sent a shaft of trepidation through Drake's gut, because he knew Ryder wasn't just amused to see him sucking face. He'd seen that before. Obviously this was something else.

He quirked a brow at his friend and Ryder chuckled. "You do like to live dangerously, don't you?" he said.

Drake narrowed his eyes. "What do you mean?"

"Kissing *her*." He nodded at Brandy.

It took a lot of effort not to bristle. How dare Ryder imply—

"She's Brandywine's daughter."

His pulse missed a beat. Drake gaped at him. Shook his head. "She's not—she's not Brandywine's daughter."

At his side Brandy stiffened.

He whipped around to stare at her. Something cold slithered through his bowels. "Brandywine's daughter's name is *Susan*."

She shrugged a shoulder. "No one calls me that."

His heart plunged. It wasn't a denial, but barely.

"Are you—" He cleared his throat. "Are you?" All he could manage.

And hell. Her head tipped. "He's my dad."

Crap.

Crap, crap, crap.

He'd fucked the commander's daughter. The *commander's* daughter! He might not be in the clutches of pirates, but he sure as shit wasn't safe.

When Brandywine found out, he'd skin him alive.

CHAPTER NINE

Brandy followed as Ryder helped Drake to sick bay, and was heartily annoyed when the orderlies wouldn't let her go in with him. "But I'm a nurse," she wailed. Apparently the stupid frog doctors didn't care.

Ryder led her to a bank of chairs in the waiting room and they sat, side by side, in silence. God. She hated waiting rooms. She always had—she never had been good at waiting—and this room was about as cold and sterile as they came. She glanced around at the soulless walls and frowned. It made her restless.

She pinned her attention on the man by her side. She hadn't noticed before—probably because his face was still slathered with camo—but he was damn attractive, easily as handsome as Drake, but in a darker way. She much preferred Drake's teasing energy to Ryder's humming intensity. It also occurred to her that as team leader, he could tell her everything that had happened on that island, but there was really only one answer she wanted at the moment.

"Did everyone get out?" she asked with no preamble. "Are they all safe?" She nearly collapsed in relief when he nodded. "And Lily?"

For some reason, his cheeks went a little pink. "Ah…Lily Wilson?"

"Yes. Is she okay?"

He glanced away. "She's fine."

"Fine?" Just fine?

"She's…with her dad right now. But I know she'll want to see you when she hears you're here."

"Good. I'd like to see her."

"Of course." He nodded, and silence fell again as she stared at the bland bulkhead and he stared at his folded fingers, but really, there was very little to talk about. Besides, she was still annoyed with him.

It also annoyed her that he turned to study her. Like a raptor observing a titmouse. Steady. Unblinking. Incessant. She felt the weight of his attention but pretended she didn't. When, at length, he didn't look away, she met his gaze. There was an odd look in his eye. His lips worked a bit, and then he finally forced out, "Does Drake really think I don't approve of him?"

She liked the thread of chagrin in his voice. That was probably the only reason she responded. "Apparently. And for some reason, all he wants is to make you proud of him."

He raked his bristly hair. "I am proud. Damn proud. Jesus."

"Maybe you should tell him that," she said softly.

"I will. If your dad doesn't kill him first."

She frowned. "My dad? Why would he kill the SEAL who rescued me?"

He tipped his head to the side. "You do remember the face-sucking, right?"

Heat crawled up her cheeks. "So? I kissed him. Why is that such a big deal?"

A grin quirked his lips. "Your dad is the *team commander*."

She remembered the look in Drake's eyes when he found out who her dad was. He'd almost seemed…scared. Which was weird. Nothing scared him. Nothing. She didn't like to think that her dad might.

But what scared her? That her father's identity might be a deal breaker for him. Yeah. That scared her to death. Funny. It had always been the other way around. Guys wanting her because of her dad's power. How ironic that now, when it really mattered, she wished that were the case.

"I still don't see why it's such a big deal." She should be able to kiss whomever the hell she wanted. It wasn't as though her father actually cared. It wasn't as though he were part of her life. It wasn't as though he wanted to be.

Ryder sighed. "There's just a code. Guys don't…kiss their buddy's sisters. Or, for God's sake, their mothers." He glanced at her. "Or their commander's daughter."

She gaped at him. "That's stupid."

"It's not. It's a code."

Brandy rolled her eyes. Men and their stupid codes.

Ryder cleared his throat. "Your dad's going to want to see you."

"He's here?" She didn't mean to squeak like that.

"Of course he's here. He's your dad."

"There's no 'of course' about it. He was never there for me when I was growing up—"

"Because your mother wanted me to stay away."

Brandy whipped around. Her heart lurched.

Her father stood in the hatch.

God, he looked old, but then, she hadn't seen him since she was twelve. His hair was gray at the temples and there were wrinkles around his eyes. He looked tired.

And it hit her, all of a sudden.

Reaction to the stress of her adventure, most likely, but more than that. At the sight of him she realized, remembered, relived how much she'd missed him. Sadness for the time they'd lost welled up in her. Sadness and reaction and relief that she was safe and he was here with her now. It came out in tears.

She hated tears on general principle, but these she could ignore. When he opened his arms to her, she stood and stepped into his embrace. It closed around her slowly, but securely. *He* was the one who clung.

"I'm so glad you're safe, Susan," he whispered into her hair. "So glad."

"I'm fine."

He held her back and studied her. Then frowned. "Don't ever scare me like that again."

"I didn't do it on purpose." She didn't intend the defiance in her response and she regretted it immediately; it always started a fight between them. They were both far too stubborn to back down...but this time, he did.

"I know. I know." He pulled her back into his arms. "We need to go. I want to get you home. Your mother's worried sick."

"I can't go." She wrestled out of his embrace.

"Why not?"

"I need to know that Drake is okay."

His brows furrowed. Also a bad sign. "Drake?"

Ryder stood. "Drake Ronan, sir." He nodded to the infirmary doors. "He's the SEAL who brought her out."

"He was shot." Brandy tangled her fingers. "They won't let me see him."

Her father snorted. "The hell they won't." He took her arm and marched her through the doors.

Unfortunate, it was, that Drake was splayed out on a gurney with his bare ass mooning everyone as a medic examined his wounds. When the medic saw her father he leaped to attention and saluted.

Drake glanced over his shoulder and cringed. "Jesus." He rolled over to hide his backside…until he realized that exposed his front. "Shit." He fumbled for a blanket to cover himself.

"At ease, Ronan," her father barked. Through his laughter.

"He's had some morphine, sir," the medic said. "So please keep that in mind as you debrief him."

Drake chuckled. "I'm already debriefed." He raised the blanket to show them. And yes, he was. He bunched his ass cheeks to give them a show.

Oh yeah. The boy was feeling no pain.

Ryder leaned in and studied the two wounds. Or one of them. "Wait. You got shot in the *ass*?" he asked.

Drake made a face. It was a weird-looking face, as though all his muscles were putty. Brandy bit back a smile. Morphine could be funny. "I got shot in the leg. *In the leg.* Twice." He glanced at her for confirmation, but there was no confirming something that was clearly visible.

"I didn't get shot once," she said, just to be helpful.

He narrowed his eyes and growled.

"Because of you, baby. You kept me safe." She waltzed over and kissed him, right there in front of everyone. Even though his eyes remained wide and trained on her father, he kissed her back. At least a little. "Daddy, this is Drake. Drake, this is Daddy."

Drake thrust out a hand but her father ignored it, though his lip curled. "We've met."

They had? She shot a questioning look at Drake; he grimaced. "I didn't know she was your daughter, sir. Honestly—"

A nasty ripple crawled up her spine. *Holy God*, she hated his tone. His words. His meaning. Most of all, she hated the retreat she sensed. Something in her chest went cold and hard—it might have been her heart—but then fury whipped through her, thawing the chill.

She firmed her jaw and forced a smile onto her face. "Drake and I are *dating*," she said baldly.

They flinched. All the men. Each and every one of them. Even the medic. She didn't care. She knew if she didn't take control of the situation here and now, Drake might use her father's rank as an escape hatch and she was not—*not*—going to allow that. If he wanted to break it off with her, it wouldn't be for the lame excuse that her dad was his boss. *By. God.*

She shot a look at her father. It might have been something of a challenging stare.

"Susan—"

"Ryder explained your stupid tradition about daughters and—"

"It's not stupid." This from Ryder.

And from her father, "It's a *code*."

"But I like Drake and he likes me." She stilled and glanced at him. "Do you still like me?"

He gazed at her like a mooncalf. A loopy mooncalf. He took her hand and gave it a noisy smooch. "Oh. Very much."

Her father made a feral noise.

"Point being, I am an adult woman and he is an adult man and, well, if we continue to see each other, I don't want you to be mean to him because of it."

"*Oh, fuck.*" Drake covered his head with the blanket. Pity that, because the move uncovered other parts of his anatomy that he might not have wanted to share.

A red tide rose on her father's cheeks. "Susan Eloise Brandywine—"

"No. Don't 'Susan Eloise' me. I'm not twelve anymore." She glowered at her father. He'd always been very domineering, especially when they butted heads. But she'd learned the art of stubbornness from the very best. "He is a wonderful man. And I really want to get to know him better. And if you give him any shit about it, I'll never speak to you again. Do you understand?"

Her father's lips worked. "Susan..."

"No one calls me Susan." No one did. Except *him*.

"I, ah..."

"Brandy."

His brow quirked. "Brandy?"

She nodded.

It was funny the way a pout formed on his face—that big bad naval commander—and he said, in a petulant voice, "But they call *me* Brandy."

Who called whom what was hardly the point. She folded her arms. "Well. What do you say? About me dating Drake?"

Her father looked down at his boots. He grimaced, but she saw it, there on his face. Acceptance. Grudging acceptance, but acceptance. His smile was pained. "Fine. But did you have to pick the squid who threw up on me?"

Brandy gasped. She whirled on Drake. He woefully peeped out from beneath the blanket. "*He's* the commander you barfed on?"

"Kinda."

The look on his face, on her father's... The visual of Drake christening her father's beloved boots... The sheer joy of being alive... It was way too much. She threw back her head and laughed.

Everything was, all of a sudden, quite wonderful.

And then, because she was so freaking happy, she gave her father another hug.

She just wouldn't tell Mom about that.

It was tough watching Brandy leave when Ryder insisted she needed to go to the chow hall and eat something; that she lingered by his side and held his hand and kissed him eased the sting. That and the fact she leaned closer and whispered, "I'll be back in a bit."

Thank God. She wasn't going anywhere.

They would be together again soon. Maybe forever, if the glint in her eye was any indication. Which was awesome, because he wanted her, needed her, loved her. Would do anything, face any adversary to have her. And she felt the same.

The realization made his soul soar.

His bubble of elation popped and dribbled out onto the floor when Commander Brandywine remained behind.

Oh. Crap.

He waited until his daughter had disappeared from sight and then turned to Drake and narrowed his eyes. "So," he said, as though that said it all. Then again, in that timbre, it might.

Drake swallowed. His mouth was suddenly dry. He had no idea

why he found this situation amusing. It was not. Must be that he was drugged out of his mind. "So," he parroted. He shouldn't have.

The commander was not amused. His brows rippled and a muscle in his cheek bunched. "You're *dating* my daughter."

"I…ah…" *Holy God.* How to respond to that? He was…more than dating her. No doubt, Brandywine wouldn't care to know the details of their "dates" up until now. In fact, if he got a whiff he might have Drake keelhauled. If they did that anymore. And if they didn't, the commander would most likely make an exception.

"Well? Are you? Dating her?"

"I would like to…sir."

"I'll just bet you would." This, of course, was muttered beneath his breath.

"Sir, she's very important to me." Granted, he never would have admitted that if he hadn't been hopped up on painkillers—not this early in their relationship—but it was the truth. It really was. She was important. She was everything.

Brandywine wasn't impressed by his declaration. He leaned in and hissed, "What my baby wants, my baby gets." He smiled like a reptile. "But if you break my daughter's heart, Ronan, I'll fucking snap you in half. Understood?"

Drake grinned; he didn't mean to and he tried not to—he should be scared shitless and appropriately intimidated—but it just happened. "Yes, sir!"

The commander pinned him with a look—that look officers gave grunts when they were about to make their lives very miserable.

Against his will, his grin widened, and then a chuckle bubbled up. It had to be the morphine, or maybe the delight that he had survived this ordeal, or his elation that Brandy was not leaving him any time soon. Or simply that he'd met her and loved her and had her. The emotions danced through his head and his heart and his soul.

Something else, however, danced in his belly. No doubt it was the effect of all those drugs on an empty stomach…but bile roiled in his gut and rose to his throat. He tried to hold it back, but he couldn't. It was an unrelenting tide of surging lava.

Brandywine's gaze locked on his face. "Ronan…"

Drake sucked in a deep breath and leaned over the side of the bed.

"Ronan…?"

He opened his mouth…

"Ronan!"

And barfed all over Brandywine's boots.

The old man leaped back with a squawk, but Drake still nailed him and nailed him good.

And for some reason, this time, it was hilarious.

EPILOGUE

"What do you think?" Lily waved to the food mounded on the dining room table—an enormous roast, several hundred chicken wings, potatoes, salads, a steaming platter of veggies, pies, cakes, and cheeses… It seemed like a lot. It seemed like way too much, but considering the crowd it needed to feed, it wasn't near enough.

Ryder's squad could put away food like nobody's business. Whenever the guys rotated off duty, they ate like the navy had starved them for three months straight.

Brandy caught her friend's eye and grinned. "We can always order pizza if we need more."

Lily laughed, a delightful trill. She'd been laughing a lot since the wedding. And, come to think of it, Ryder hadn't been such a gruff ass since he'd made Lily an honest woman. It was obvious the two were meant to be together. Brandy's gaze flicked from Lily's glowing face, to her soft blonde curls, to the baby bump pushing out her jumper, and something warmed in her heart. Though that nightmare on an island off Somalia had been horrific for both of them, there was no denying that week—had it only been a year ago?—had changed all their lives. For the better.

Lily had found Ryder and Brandy had found—

A roar rose in the living room and Brandy peeked through the door to where the guys were watching the game. It was an intimidating collection of testosterone. Ryder and Tate were quibbling about a call the ref had made, while Garrett and Luke egged them on. Mason sat in the corner easy chair looking on with a smile on his lips and a beer in his hand. They were all drop-dead gorgeous, but it was Drake who captured her attention.

Drake, with his laughing eyes and his beautiful smile. His evil dimples and that tantalizing scruff… God, he was beautiful. It was so wonderful to have him home. Safe.

She couldn't wait to tell him—

He looked up just then and their gazes clashed. A sear of excitement whipped through her. When he stood and prowled toward her, her pulse shot into high gear. Even now, after all this time, he had this effect on her.

He sidled up to her and wrapped her in his arms. She let him. "Hey, baby." His kiss was delicious.

"Hey, you. How's the game?"

He shrugged. "Who cares? When you're in my line of vision I can't—"

Another roar rose and he instinctively glanced at the TV…then he forced his gaze back to her. She smiled and tugged him into the kitchen while Lily nibbled her grin and headed to Ryder's side with another beer. Lily always knew when to give them their privacy. Such a friend.

The door swung shut on them and the sounds of the game—and the ribaldry—receded. Drake yanked her close again, kissed her again. Something hard nudged her hip. "Mmm. I missed you." She rubbed against him and he winced and shifted to the right.

"I missed you too." The kisses deepened, lingered, and then to her annoyance, he eased away, his features fixed in a somber arrangement, one that made something ripple in her gut. "You know, Brandy…" He stalled. His lips worked. His Adam's apple bobbed. Then he started again. "You know, Brandy, we've been dating for over a year."

"Mmm hmm." More than just dating—all his shit was at her house—but, whatever.

"And we spend all our time together when I'm not in the field."

"Mmm hmm."

"And your dad kind of likes me now." *Kind of.*

She nestled closer and kissed his neck. He sighed and gently eased her away again. She frowned at him because she wanted to be close. Ached to be close. But when she leaned toward him, he stepped back and shoved his hand into his pocket.

When he pulled out a velvet-covered box, her heart skipped.

Was that...?

She gaped at him. A red flush rose on his cheeks. "I... Brandy... Will you..." He snapped open the lid and her breath snagged. The flash of a gorgeous diamond ring completely distracted her attention. "Will you marry me?" When she continued to stare, speechless, he lifted a shoulder. "Might as well."

She narrowed her eyes and gored him with a ferocious glare. It was difficult, because she wanted to dance and sing and fart rainbows.

"Might. As. Well?"

"Aw shit, baby." He raked his fingers through his hair, or what there was of it. "I'm sorry I'm not some romantic, studly guy..." *Oh, he was studly.* "But I love you and you love me, and I can't think of anyone else I'd rather spend my life with. Besides..." He put out a lip. "I need you."

Seriously? There was no call for whining. Groveling, maybe, but not whining.

"I would love to marry you, Drake," she said in a no-nonsense tone, and when he started to squeal, she lifted a quelling finger. "But..."

It was adorable the way his expression fell. "But?"

"I made a vow to myself when I was twelve. It was a sacred vow."

"When you were twelve?"

"Yes."

"What did you vow?"

"I swore never to marry a squid."

A smile cracked his face and he tucked her closer, so their bodies were flush and warm and melded against each other. "But you fell in love with a squid, baby." He kissed her to prove it.

And crap, she had.

With kisses like that, she could never deny him anything, and he knew it. "Marry me," he commanded and kissed her again. "Marry me, marry me, marry me." Each demand punctuated with a kiss on her nose, her forehead, her chin.

"Good glory, but you are insistent."

He grinned. His dimples blossomed. "I'm a SEAL. You know we never give up. You might as well surrender."

She looped her arms around his neck and leaned against him and gusted a sigh. "Oh, all right. I suppose."

He perked right up at that. "You will? You'll marry me?"

"I sup-pose."

He responded with yet another kiss, but this one was all wet and smoochy and not seductive in the slightest. When he lifted his head, he said, "We should go tell the guys."

She tugged him back down. "Not yet. There's something I need to—" A flutter in her midsection stalled her words. She stilled. Her breath hung. Since she was pressed against him, he felt it too. He had to.

His gaze bored into hers. "What was that?" he asked, although in some part of his mind, he probably already knew.

She blinked innocently. "I dunno. Aliens maybe?"

The flutter rippled again, and again. In the last few months, since he'd been gone, it had become more and more frequent. Each time it sent a trickle of happiness through her.

Slowly, his gaze drifted down her body to her belly, assessing. Then he nudged her, measuring the girth of her tummy. The grin, when it came, was slow and sexy, a glorious unfurling of his delight. "Oh my God," he said.

"Oh my God," she confirmed.

"When?"

"July?"

He stared at her, his eyes wide, his mouth agape. "Oh my God." A whisper.

"Are you happy?" She didn't know why she felt the need to ask, other than she really wanted the confirmation.

He cupped her cheeks and kissed her once more, this time reverently. "Never been happier, baby. Never."

Neither of them made mention of the tiny tear in the corner of his eye, but Brandy kissed it away.

No need for tears.

Not today.

Today was a good day.

And all the rest would be too.

ABOUT THE AUTHOR

Her Royal Hotness, Sabrina York, is the New York Times and USA Today Bestselling author of hot, humorous stories for smart and sexy readers. Her titles range from sweet & sexy to scorching romance. Visit her webpage at www.sabrinayork.com to check out her books, excerpts and contests.

BOOKS BY SABRINA YORK

CONTEMPORARY ROMANCE

Heartbreak on a Stick
Stone Hard SEALs

Tryst Island Series
Rebound, Book 1
Dragonfly Kisses, Book 2
Smoking Holt, Book 3
Heart of Ash, Book 4
Devlin's Dare, Book 5
Parker's Passion, Book 6

Wired Series
Adam's Obsession, Book 1
Tristan's Temptation, Book 2
Making Over Maris, Book 3

REGENCY ROMANCE

Untamed Highlander Series (Coming Soon!)
Hannah and the Highlander
Susana and the Scot
Lana and the Laird

Noble Passions Series
Folly, Book 1
Dark Fancy, Book 2
Dark Duke, Book 3
Brigand, Book 4
Defiant, Book 5

FANTASY ROMANCE

Lust Eternal

ANTHOLOGIES AND COLLECTIONS

Come Hell or High Water (12 Alarm Cowboy Collection)
Five Alarm Fire (High Octane Heroes)
A Cowboy for Delilah (Cowboy Heat)
Saving Charlotte (Smokin' Hot Firemen)
Sterling's Seduction (Elite Metal Collection)
Tarnished Honor (The Incomparables: Waterloo Hero Collection)
The Real McCoy (Cowboy 12 Pack Collection)
Whipped (WTRAFSOG #8 Collection)

SHORT STORIES AND NOVELLAS

Extreme Couponing
Fierce
Pushing Her Buttons
Man Hungry
Rising Green (Horror)
Snow Angels
Training Tess
Trickery

www.ingramcontent.com/pod-product-compliance
Lightning Source LLC
Chambersburg PA
CBHW071910220626

47052CB00002B/285